Hot Sizzling Erotica

PLAY HOUSE

AMY REDEK

I0547734

About the Publisher
4Fun Publishing, a member of **BLVNP Incorporated**, 340 S. Lemon #6200, Walnut CA 91789, info@blvnp.com / legal@blvnp.com
NOTE: Due to the highly emotional reaction of some people to works of erotic fiction, any email sent to the above address that contains foul language or religious references is automatically deleted by our anti-spam software and will not be seen. All other communications are welcome.

DISCLAIMER
Please don't be stupid and kill yourself. This book is a work of FICTION. Do not try any new sexual practice that you find in this book. It is fiction and not to be confused with reality. Neither the author nor the publisher or its associates assume any responsibility for any loss, injury, death or legal consequences resulting from acting on the contents in this book. Every character in this book is over 18 years of age. The author's opinions are not to be construed as the opinions of the publisher. The material in this book is for entertainment purposes ONLY. Enjoy.

PLAY HOUSE
Hot Sizzling Erotica

By: Amy Redek

ISBN: 978-1-62761-849-6

My name is Danny Rundene and I live in a big house in a mid-west town with my parents and four siblings--two older brothers and two sisters. I'm the fourth child with a sister as the youngest in the family. We're not rich but neither are we poor for dad works in an aircraft components plant while mom works in the canteen of the same company. She is now the head cook and runs the place very well. With my brothers being four and five years older than me, they tend to keep to each other and did not mind me, which made me turn to Peter Denton, who was my age and lived just three houses down from us in Beech Avenue. He lives on a big estate near the aircraft plant. Each company house sits on an acre of land that surrounded the plant. All the roads that ran east to west were named after trees while those north and south were of late Presidents.

So I would spend most of my free time at Peter's house while also taking the time to be a regular mischievous kid that most boys are prone to be. Peter was the only son of George and Alice Denton, who could no longer bear more children because of a problem while giving birth. The Dentons were quite pleased that Peter and I get along well and I often sleep over their house. Like ours, the Denton residence had five bedrooms so one of the empty ones became our playroom when we were little, especially in the winter when we couldn't play outside.

With both of our dads plus my mom, working at the plant, we got to go to the Christmas party that the company throws every year for the children of their employees. We were also given guided tours of the plant, which totally fascinated Peter seeing work done on the floor from the making of the designs that we saw in the offices. This prompted him to become involved in doing some designing himself while I was taken by the way the workers turned these drawings into components for aircraft.

Now I wasn't academically the brightest in our class but had a gift hands, woodworking and the like. I built quite a library of 'Do It Yourself' books, which I virtually knew by heart. Peter was the brainy one between us and used to get quite a lot of bright ideas that got us into trouble. The usual things for two young boys but we were tolerated. He also was good at drawing, though I should really say designs, and it looked as if he had a future in being a designer whereas I could become a handyman.

This showed when I was about 12. Our house was on the corner of Beech Avenue and Lincoln Avenue. The wall on the side of Lincoln Avenue was knocked down one night, when a car bounced off the said wall. About three meters was knocked down, most of which fell into our garden. Dad was furious at this and took photos of the demolished wall and sent them off to our insurance company. They came back with a letter telling us to have it repaired and they would foot the bill as long as it was within reason. Now some of the quotes were quite high and I somehow managed to talk dad into letting me rebuild the wall using the bricks that could be salvaged and I would get some of the money for the job.

So with dad buying the cement and sand, I cleaned up each brick and found that these can be put back without having to buy any extras. It took me a week to mix the mortar and lay the bricks and even if I say so myself, I did a bloody good job of it, getting praised by both mom and dad at an excellent job even when I was only 10 years old. Dad put in a bill along with some photos of the wall during its reconstruction and the finished wall. The insurance company paid up without any trouble, so I got a hefty slice from dad for the work that I had put into.

The following year, mom went mad when she saw me up on our roof replacing some tiles that had been blown off because of strong winds, but I did another good job and it looked as if this was to be my profession when I grew older, a handyman. I used some of the money from the wall building, to build what we would call a workshop at Peter's garden. His parents put some money in the project too, when they saw the design Peter had drawn to show what we were building. This was because he had become fascinated with model planes and would design his own and so he wanted a place for me to help him in the building of these planes.

Peter's dad was against me building what would be the workshop, but agreed after Peter had shown him the wall that I had rebuilt. For lighting the workshop as it was being built, Peter and I dug a trench two foot deep and six inches wide, from the house to put in the conduit with the wires inside. When George, Peter's dad, found out that it was me that had put the electricity in, really kicked up and called in a qualified electrician to check out what I had done. Boy, didn't I feel smug when the guy said that he couldn't have done a better job, even the putting in of a trip switch which many people didn't do. So we were allowed to carry on with the building and with the roof on, Peter began putting what was needed inside, a big table for him to do his designs and two others for me to cut and shape the balsa wood and put these together according to his design. We even put a sofa in there too, as well as pictures of girls up on the walls for decoration. Though the girls on the photo were clothe, some were still showing quite a bit of tit.

We were 15 years old when this was completed and some evenings, we would smuggle in some girly magazines and with these open in front of us as we sat on the sofa, we would do what boys do at our age. At this age, we had moved on to the high school where Peter's mom was a teacher for the subjects English and History. The latter being mostly of America and of famous people who had brought our country into being. To her credit, she still didn't favour us over any of the others in our class.

I was now sleeping over at Peter's house at least twice a week with some of the work we had been doing in building the workshop and quite often we would sleep in the same bed. But now I began to have questions about Peter with the choice of pictures that he would cut out of the magazines that we got our hands on. I had been making frames for these cutouts, using clear plastic sheeting instead of glass, hanging them on the wall. These were of girls but Peter was cutting out pictures of men showing their erections and giving blow jobs. These were put into the frames and those of the girls were on the opposite side. There were pictures of men having anal sex that made me wonder which way Peter was going. Where I would have pictures of girls and their tits showing for me to do what boys do, he would have those of men giving blow jobs when he did the same.

I spent more of my time at Peter's house working in the workshop after school and over the weekends, as I have already said, cutting the balsa wood to his specifications while he was gluing the parts together before we put in the engine. These were radio controlled and we would take the finished plane down to the mall on a Sunday to use the empty car park to fly the plane.

We crashed the first four planes, working out what went wrong and making corrections after each crash, until we had one that took off from the tarmac okay and did its turns in the air, much to our delight. But upon landing, which look good at first but then flipped over. It took two weeks to get the correct weight at the rear end to keep it down, and upon landing, and we were over the moon when it finally landed perfectly every time that it flew.

We were on a high that night while having dinner at his house, him being able to regale his mom and dad with what we had achieved. His exuberance carried over to the bedroom that I slept in with him coming in to get into bed with me.

'What a day,' he said and I could hear the enthusiasm in his voice as he stroked my naked chest. We both now slept in the raw not wearing constricting pyjamas, which were uncomfortable to wear when you had a hard on. We've cracked the weight problem and can now make bigger ones, God, it was so exciting and he lay on my chest as he kissed me. I can't have been shocked for my arms had gone round him and held him tight as we kissed for several minutes before breath was needed by both of us. I could feel his heart still pounding away in his chest and I'm sure that he felt mine doing the same.

Now that we were really into making models that worked, whether these were planes or ships, I would spend most of my time with Peter making these models and sleeping over five nights a week.

During the day after school, we would work on making our planes and slowly proceed on to make other mobile toys and at night, he would give me a kiss before we went to sleep.

Time marched on with both of us, doing well at school and even starting to sell some of our models as we seemed to be turning out even better ones as we went along, when decisions had to be made as to our future. This was where Peter and I would part for he would be going off to a university to study more on designing.

With us both reaching 18 and no longer considered boys but young men, growing at the prescribed rate that nature had intended for us. We both grew more in height and it pleased me to find that my cock had also gotten bigger over that year, more so than Peter's. We had finished high school when disaster struck! Not me or Peter, but it had a later profound effect on me. His father had an accident at work. It wasn't because of his inattention to his work but to a faulty piece of machinery. He had been working at a metal lathe when it disintegrated under his hand and pieces of the shrapnel, which is about the only way to describe the pieces of metal that came apart, almost severed his left hand. It was later proven that the accident was really caused by faulty machinery.

He was rushed off to the hospital where they at least saved his hand but couldn't repair the damage done and so would have no use of that hand for the rest of his life. They operated on it three times but couldn't repair the muscles or nerves over a period of a month. With the experts proving it was the machine components' fault, he was immediately granted a disability pension and with him being unable to work any longer at what he was used to, he was offered a position as a security officer, and took over as the senior night officer. Since it was the night shift, his pay was made up to be what he had been earning on the floor, so financially, he didn't lose out.

So it really wasn't a calamity for him but it became a bonus for me, for when things of nearly any nature that had to be done at Peter's house, I stepped into the breach and did the odd jobs that his father could no longer do. My parents had no objection to me sleeping over at Peter's house five nights a week and were pleased that with the jobs I did that George couldn't do, I refused any payment because they fed me when I did sleep over, so everybody was happy with this arrangement.

But the accident had affected Peter, for with his father in the hospital just after it had happened, he would cry in bed at night where I would then take him into my arms to comfort him. I would brush away his tears and didn't stop him from kissing me and I suppose I should have been shocked when he began stroking my chest and stomach, his hand also touching my cock.

'Danny? Can....can I do what the men do in my pictures?' he asked, a slight stammer in his voice. This would be one of those with a man holding another man's erection and with the head of the cock in his mouth.

'If you want to,' I said, my heart beat having increased at the thought, seeing the picture in my mind, my cock now really throbbing as his hand moved slowly up and down on my erection with a firm grip. He kept hold of me, still moving his hand up and down on my cock as he slithered down the bed and felt his head rest on my stomach and his breath wafting over the head just before he took it into his hot mouth. It was hot and I gave out a gasp at the incredible feeling that ran through my body as I felt the suction had the foreskin pushed back with his lips so that the bare flesh was now being stroked by his tongue. My body had gone rigid at first but now started to relax at the pleasure that flowed throughout me as he worked away in both the tonguing and sucking of my erection.

With it being the first time that my cock had been sucked upon, I soon felt my balls reacting and had my cum shoot up the tube of my penis and erupt inside his mouth making his head jerk at the force that it came out of the eye of my cock. Not once, twice or three times but six shots of my cum spewed its way into his mouth and I'm sure I heard him slobber as he tried to suck and swallow my emission. My thighs had tightened up just before I came and now with my balls being empty, they relaxed and I gave out a groan at the pleasure Peter had just given me in the sucking and jerking while taking the whole load of cum to swallow.

He carried on for another couple of minutes, squeezing my cock in the upward movement of his hand until he lifted his head off of me and I felt that the air that wafted over the bare flesh of my cock seemed quite cold as compared to the heat it had been experiencing. I then had another surprise, for after he had moved back up the bed, he lay half on my chest as he kissed me. I can't have been shocked for my arms had gone round him and held him tight as we kissed for several minutes before breath was needed by both of us. I could feel his heart still pounding away in his chest and I'm sure that he felt mine doing the same.

'Danny! That was incredible! I never thought it would be as good as that,' he panted, his eyes shining in the gloom of the room.

'Neither did I,' I replied, still holding him in my arms, my mind still swirling with the pleasure I had received, then was given another jolt.

'Will you suck on me now?' Peter asked.

Fucking hell was the thought that flashed in my brain and found my mouth speaking before really giving it thought.

'Yes, Peter,' and had him kiss me again which was nearly as good as having my cock sucked before he broke off and rolled over onto his back. Now was my moment of truth as I slowly moved up onto an elbow and reached down and found his hard erection lying up on his stomach and held it upright as I moved down the bed to have it just in front of my face. I could feel it throbbing away and hoped that I would be as good in sucking his cock.

I unconsciously licked my lips before opening my mouth and lowered my head down and took in the head of his cock. It was hot on my tongue and managed, as he had done, in pushing the foreskin down so that I had the bare flesh to run my tongue over as I began to suck on my first cock. It was hard in my grip and somehow felt different as the soft skin moved easily up and down over the hard and solid muscle that was inside as opposed to the normal jerking off of him as we had done in the past. But then found that I was enjoying having his cock there for me to suck and tease the G-spot with my tongue, making his body quiver as I did so.

I then knew just how a baby felt with a pacifier in its mouth to suck and not having teeth, to squeeze it with the gums not realising that it was swallowing its own saliva. I think it is this act as a baby makes men and women love to suck on an erect penis for it was how they were kept quiet when in their crib, sucking on this piece of rubber which was exactly how it felt having Peter's cock in my mouth. A rubber pacifier that made me feel good and young again. The difference being that I could hold the shaft of this lovely cock and move my hand up and down to get what the baby didn't, and that was his sperm.

I felt Peter's thighs tighten up and knew that he was reaching his peak and I squeezed it harder and moved my hand faster as he began to groan and I felt the cock swell a little bit more and had him cum in my mouth. It felt like my mouth had a bucket full as the last shot joined the rest and with my lips clamped tight round the head, moved his cum about, getting the slightly salty taste on my tongue before swallowing it and then continued to suck on the bare flesh of the head to clean off any remains of his cum.

He gave out a big sigh as his body relaxed and I felt his fingers move gently through the hair on my head as his cock softened slightly having now given up his cum. With a final chew, I then released him and gave the head of his cock a kiss before moving back up the bed and into his open arms and we kissed again.

That was our first time sucking on each other's cock and it was an experience that I would never forget and we would repeat this as often as we could, be it in bed or in the workshop. We would kiss each other and fumble the erection out of the trousers or shorts to suck and gently chew and then have the aphrodisiac of our cum to taste and savour before swallowing.

Now that we were really into making models that worked, whether these were planes or ships, I would spend most of my time with Peter making these models and sleeping over five nights a week and it must have been two weeks after our first act of oral sex that Peter now wanted to move on to having anal sex. I was very dubious about this knowing that if I fucked him, he would want to fuck me. So it began with me using a finger or two up his backside as we played with each other in bed and found that he loved being fingered by me. He then began to do the same to me but not only that, he would even tongue my ring piece which was quite exciting and I eventually got round to rimming him too.

Peter tried all over the house to try and find if his dad had some condoms and it was a few years later we learned why he didn't have any, which I will share in time. So Peter bought some from the pharmacy in town and got two ready on the night we were going to begin having anal sex. He'd also bought a couple tubes of lube having heard or read that this aided the entry of the cock into an asshole.

He wanted to be fucked first and so after a few sucks on my erection, he rolled a condom down over my cock and squeezed some lube out over my covered cock's head and also a fingerful to his ass as he lay on his back with his legs in the air for me to get in between them. I shuffled forward on my knees, my rubber-covered cock bouncing up and down until I had his legs up on my shoulders. I could see his puckered asshole with the lube around it and guided my cock to this place and felt him give out a tremor as it was put in place.

His eyes were shining as he looked up at me and had a sickly looking grin on his face as I put my hands around his thighs as I began to slowly move myself forward.

'Slowly. Slowly,' he grunted as he began to feel the pressure of my cock trying to widen his ass.

'Is it hurting you?' I asked, pausing in my pushing.

'A little, but if you move slowly and take your time, it should be okay,' he grunted.

'Well if you relax yourself, it shouldn't hurt then,' I said, knowing by the feel around the half of the head of my cock being in his ass, his sphincter muscle was trying to stop me from entering.

'I'm trying to,' he grunted, a spasm of pain crossed his face and all of a sudden, the head of my cock was inside him feeling the heat of his body's interior and his face broke out into a grin. 'It feels bigger than it looks, but I'm okay now.'

So I eased myself forward some more until I could go no farther with my throbbing cock, my thighs pressing his bum cheeks. Now with me being fully inside him, I began to move myself, fucking his ass and finding out that I loved the tightness that surrounded my cock as it slid back and forth due to the aid of the lube.

'This is great, Danny,' he gasped with a big smile on his face. 'Fucking awesome!' I thought so too as I fucked him, feeling his muscle flexing itself around my shaft as though it was trying to stop me from moving, but found out later at it was a natural body reaction to having an intruder there.

'Too right, Peter!' I grunted as I began to move myself faster inside him as I approached my peak, really ramming my hips hard up at him as I then began to shoot my load out into the condom. I was breathing hard as I came to a halt, letting his legs slide down my arms and fell forward to kiss him. His arms came round my shoulders as I lay on top of him, my cock still buried deep in his ass.

'That was fantastic, Danny,' he said with that big grin on his face. 'You'll enjoy it.'

Will I? This was my thought as I felt myself sliding out of him because of his body relaxing, almost forcing me out and causing him to give out a groan at the loss of my still throbbing cock.

'Let me suck on you,' he said, heaving his body up to roll me off of him to finish up on my back. He was quickly up onto his knees and pulled the condom off and dived down to take as much of my still hard cock into his mouth to suck and pull out any cum still inside. He also licked off the residue that had coated the head, poking his tongue into the eye of my cock in the process which made me squirm a little. 'You do taste nice,' he said as he came up to half lay on me, kissing me with his sperm covered lips and used his tongue to push against my teeth until they parted and our tongues began to talk to each other. I could feel his hard erection pressing up against my thigh and knew that he was going to ask to use it inside me. I wasn't wrong.

'Oh, Danny. Let me fuck you now! I need the same relief and you'll enjoy it, I promise,' he said.

'It won't hurt, will it?' I managed to ask between his kisses.

'I'd be telling a lie if I said it didn't, but not a lot, and only at the beginning and it soon goes. Besides, my cock's not as big as yours. It only hurts a little at the start and once the head's inside, it's great and you'll enjoy it. That I promise,' he said.

'But you looked so uncomfortable being bent in the middle,' I said.

'Then we'll do it doggie fashion like in some of my pictures.' This position wasn't the only other one he had saved to look at. Another way was both men lying on their sides with the recipient having one leg in the air as he was fucked and also two men having sex while the giver was sitting on a chair with the man getting fucked was astride and sitting on the thighs of the man doing it.

'Be gentle with me then,' I said, 'and take it slow.'

'Well, I found that if you relax yourself, it would be easier,' he said.

Huh! Relax! That I found hard to do, but he rolled off of me and grabbed a condom, sat back on his heels and rolled the rubber down over his upright cock. I then rolled over onto my front and got myself up onto my knees with him now behind me. I flinched as I felt his finger rub some lube into my asshole and waited with a beating heart for the first time to have a cock pushed up inside me. Then I felt both of his knees nudging my ankles indicating that I should move them farther apart. This I did, the bed slightly bouncing to our movements and his left hand came up onto my hip as he shuffled that bit closer and I flinched again when the head of his cock nestled to the lube that was around my ring piece.

I tried my hardest to relax myself as the pressure on my ass increased with him leaning forward as his other hand came up to my other hip to pull me backwards onto his rampant cock. The first half inch of it was equivalent to two of his fingers, but another quarter of it was like three fingers. Boy, I thought he was using his fist as the rest of the head of his cock widened my asshole and I gave out a cry, which made him pause with the head half inside me.

'Christ! That hurts,' I cried while on my hands and knees though I learned later that it was better to support myself on my elbows with my head down onto the pillow.

'Then relax yourself, you stupid sod,' he cried out and gave a hefty slap to the cheek of my bum. That jolted me and at the same time, the head of his cock moved inside me.

'Wow!' I cried, now feeling that head inside me, throbbing away to his heartbeat.

'It gets better,' I heard him say as the rest of his cock slid up into me until his thighs came up tight to the cheeks of my bum and he could go no farther. It was incredible having the whole length of him inside me, not only throbbing, but pulsating away as he made it twitch causing my muscle that was there inside me to start flexing itself against the intrusive shaft.

'Yes,' I managed to get out in a strangled voice as he began moving himself back and forth, having his throbbing cock creating all kinds of emotions to flood through my body. I can't describe them as there was so many that flashed through me in that microsecond as his cock now really began to plough the virgin meadow of my backside. I found I was even dribbling at the mouth at all these feelings that coursed through my body as he fucked me and really began to revel in the thrill that he was giving me. I couldn't help but give out the odd grunt at a really hard inward thrust of his cock and found myself moving my ass back onto him as he pushed forward. My body positively glowed at the pleasure I was receiving as his cock smoothed out the kinks in my canal, pulsating and throbbing at the same time as he moved.

It was feeling his fingers start digging onto my hips to pull me back onto him that told me he was very close to giving me his load, albeit, into a condom. He had the first of a full thrust as he began shooting out his cum, filling the rubber as he ground his hips up tight to my bum, feeling the head of his cock increasing in size at each shot. Christ! He had shot me to the moon and I was in heaven having his throbbing cock give me so much pleasure and thrill just being where it was and the jerking as he came.

I had been gasping at every emission of his seed and now he was really panting for breath as he came to a halt and leaned over onto my back, letting me feel his racing hearbeat as sweat from his forehead dropped onto my back, his cock still throbbing inside me.

My arms gave way and I fell forward onto the bed with him now fully on top of me with his cock still buried in my ass, feeling not only the throbbing but his hot panting breath on my neck as he kissed me there. My sphincter muscle was flexing itself away at twice the rate of his throbbing cock, simply revelling in the thrill I had been given and with him still stuck up inside me.

There were multiple groans from the both of us as he slowly eased himself up off of my back and felt his cock begin to slide out of me, my muscle trying its utmost to hold and keep that throbbing lump of flesh inside me, but he won, and I felt my ring piece slightly widen itself as the head of his cock left me. I nearly cried at this loss but managed to control myself as he lifted himself full up off of me and with me now bereft of his cock, rolled over onto my side to see that he was quite red in the face but with that big grin.

'How was that then, lover?' he asked looking down at me.

'Great, Peter! Fucking great!' I managed to get out as I moved myself down to strip off that condom and take the wet and sperm-covered cock into my mouth to suck out the residue of his cum and clean up the head with my tongue. 'Are we now really lovers, Peter?'

'Yes, Danny,' he said, pulling me up into an embrace. 'We are lovers,' and he kissed me.

I didn't think it possible that us two could be lovers at our age, both being of the same sex, but with a shiver of delight conceded that we were indeed lovers. We had each taken the seed of each other into our mouths and had now actually consummated this love by fucking each other.

Peter too was most pleased as we could then continue in our love-making at night as well as during the weekend in the workshop.

Many times, we would pack up working and strip off our clothes and either suck on each other's cock or have a mutual fucking session. It was some time later that I found out that Alice, Peter's mother, had actually seen us fucking in the workshop by looking through the window. She had also seen us at odd times during the night, just looking in to see if we were okay and seeing us both asleep, naked, and in each other's arms.

Peter's father had been in the hospital for a month but was now back home and looking forward to his new job as a security guard, the senior one at that on the night shift.

This was where Peter and I parted. Not in sexual love between but of our academic status. With him being that much brighter than me, he opted to enrol in a university to study artistic designing whereas I decided to leave school and began to be self-employed as a handyman.

Word had already gone around the neighbourhood that I was a dab hand at anything and soon began to get lots of requests to do repairs, small constructions, whatever. The fact that my pricing of jobs was nearly always below the competition's meant less time spent working with Peter's designs in the work shop. But we managed over that summer holiday period before he had to move off to his university.

Now I don't know if it was deliberate or not, but as soon as Peter went off, Alice had a multitude of jobs for me to do around the house and grounds. It might appear with my story so far that our parents didn't have much contact, but it's wrong for there were weekends that we would dine at each other's house and had a good time as we all got along well with each other. Now with Peter being away, I would still sleep over in his house to do some kind of work there. Alice insisted that I stayed and had dinner with her, what with her husband George now working the night shift in his security job. She said that she enjoyed my company and it made her feel not so lonely having a male sleeping there overnight. She would cook dinner for two and breakfast for three when George came home in the morning.

It was on my second night of sleeping over that Alice came into the room that I slept in. I wasn't prepared for this when she entered .

'Move over, Danny,' she said, having come in while I was still awake and she pulled the top cover off and got into bed with me. The light in the room was off but I could still see that she was naked as she slipped off her gown and had her bare flesh come in contact with mine. 'I am so lonely at night with George being at work and just want someone to cuddle with before I go to sleep, missing this part for the past couple of months.'

I was gob smacked at having her in bed with me while both of us were naked, which left me speechless and so could not make any comment at that moment.

'Hold me, Danny,' she said, feeling her turn on her side to me, feeling the naked flesh of her breast against my chest and automatically moved my arms so that she could snuggle up close to me, that tit now pressing itself tighter to me. 'This is what I've been missing. Having a man's arms around me in bed.' Man! I was still a boy in reality, and here she was saying that I was a man.

'A big man in all senses of the word,' she breathed into my ear. 'Many nights I've looked into your room, or Peter's if it comes to that, seeing the pair of you naked, lying in each other's arms and both having erections.' Her hand was now stroking my chest. 'I've also seen you and Peter making love in your workshop and would like to have what he has been having over the past month.' I was still speechless at what she was saying as her hand moved down from my chest and found that I was indeed fully erect. Well what young man wouldn't get a massive hard on if a naked female had gotten into his bed. 'I've been wanting to hold this for all those times for you really are big and I have the need of any woman, especially holding what I've now got in my hand. Oh Danny, make love and fuck me!' It took me a moment or two to try and get things straight in my head. Here was Alice. Wife of George and the mother of Peter, knowing that Peter and I had fucked each other and now she wants me to do the same to her. Now you with dirty minds think that she was referring to fucking her up the ass, but I knew that a woman had another place for an erect cock and that being her vagina.

'A…A…Alice,' I stuttered. I had been told years ago that I was to always call her by her given name and not as Mrs. Denton. 'We…we can't. You're married!'

'At this moment, that has nothing to do with that. You are a man and have got an erect and hard cock. I am a woman that needs that solid piece of flesh,' her hand now holding my erection in a firm grip and moving the soft skin up and down over the hard muscle that it covered. I blurted out the only thing I could think off at the time.

'I haven't got any condoms.'

'A condom's not needed Danny,' she said softly. 'I had difficulty in birthing Peter, I had to have my uterus removed, so no more children for me.'

'But... but you're married to George,' I stuttered again.

'George is not here, but you are, and you've got what I need,' she replied, still in that soft voice, one that only here, in this bedroom, had I ever heard her speak like this.

'But you've said that you've seen Peter and I......' I had to break off the ending of saying that we had fucked each other up the ass.

'That's two young men together. Quite normal in most cases, but now is your time to have sex with a woman,' she breathed. With her hand moving up and down on my erection and her tit moving alongside my chest, I was lost. Lost in what I now know was lust. A naked woman in bed with me, rubbing my cock and wanting me to fuck her; mother of Peter and wife to George, that phrase had no meaning now. She gave out a groan and I turned as much as I could towards her and found her mouth with mine and we kissed.

She knew she had won and pulled me so that I was then on top of her as she rolled onto her back and now had both of her full breasts being squashed by my chest, my erection hard up between our stomachs. I felt her legs open and with a little push of my shoulders, I felt my cock slide down between those open legs and felt the wetness of her pussy through the head of my now really throbbing cock.

'Oh, Alice,' I murmured between our lips as I moved my body up a little and had my cock begin to slide up into the hot interior of her body. Her legs came up to my sides and pulled me even closer to her as my cock, unerring, found its own way into her until our pubes came together and I was fully inside that heated oven that was there.

'Yes Danny, yes,' she breathed into my mouth and I then carried on and fucked Peter's mother. As I slid my cock back and forth inside her, I couldn't help but notice the difference between the slackness of her vagina to the tightness of Peter's ass, but what the fuck! A hole was a hole and I was doing just that.

With it being my first time having sex with a woman, it could only have been a minute at the most when I began to give her my sperm, heaving my body into hers and letting my throbbing cock send it up into her at its own pace until I had emptied my balls inside her.

She had been giving out little cries of delight at every shot of my seed and I had been groaning at every pulsating shot having risen up with my arms outstretched alongside her body as my hips were the only other part of my body moving, plus my cock up inside her as I came. Now, panting heavily, I slowly collapsed onto the cushions of her chest as her legs came down by my sides and her arms now squeezed me tight to her hot body.

'I needed that Danny, thank you,' she breathed, almost panting like I was, for I could feel her chest moving rapidly under my chest as well as her heart beat.

'But I came to soon,' I managed to get out in one breath, still trying to get more air into my lungs.

'That was to be expected with it being your first time with a woman. But it will only get better with more experience,' she said, her hands moving up and pulling my head down to kiss me. 'I know you enjoyed sucking on Peter's cock and having him suck on yours, and now

I would like to suck on it and get the same pleasure that you both shared in sucking one another.'

Again I was speechless at her wanting to suck on me even though my cock was still up hard and throbbing inside her as she began to ease me down from lying on top of her. I gave out a groan with her little mew as my cock slid out and had her roll me over onto my back, the covering sheet being taken with me and now was crumpled up on the other side of me.

Now I knew that a limpet was a mollusc and it adhered itself to rocks and a limpet mine was an explosive device that was attached to the hull of a ship to explode and cripple it. But I didn't know that this could be applied to a female mouth as hers, on moving down on me, could come under that name as she did that very thing by clamping herself to my cock.

The grip that her lips had made below the head of my cock would have defied all attempts to remove it as she sucked and tongued the head of it. All I could do was give out a groan as she sucked not only any sperm left inside my cock, but of her own juices that had coated it with her hand moving up and down, squeezing anything left inside me. In fact, she was also teaching me how to suck on an erect and hard cock. Boy, won't Peter be surprised the next time I got to suck on him with me copying how his mother sucked on me.

I gave out a gasp as she released me to feel the cool air move over the bared flesh of my erection that I now felt starting to deflate.

'What a lovely cock you have, Danny' she said as she came back up to half lay on me, a tit being squashed against my chest. 'I can't wait for it to rise again and give me what I really want.'

'What…what more can I give you?' I stammered, wondering what the hell was she wanting now.

'An orgasm! It's been ages since my last one, and you've got the cock that could do that,' she said between her kisses to me. I was still in a world of disbelief as I held her in my arms, having her kissing me and I was reciprocating. Now I had heard that an orgasm for a woman was the equivalent of a male ridding himself of his semen, which to Peter and I, it was cumming. So how the hell do you get to give a woman and orgasm as she had said without fucking her? If it had been ages since her last one, what was George, her husband, doing wrong was my thought at this conundrum. I was just about to find out the answer after I asked her how.

'That's simple,' she replied. 'I've just been down and sucked on you, though this was just after you had your orgasm. The art is to bring the woman up to her orgasm by going down on her before penetration.' This struck me as being odd and you can now see why I didn't do very well in school, for I didn't really understand what she was saying evident in what I said next.

'But you haven't got a cock for me to suck on,' was what I had said, and later realised that she could have really torn me to pieces with that inane remark. But remember, she was a teacher at her school and knew exactly how to answer the question without belittling me in the process.

'Well you've just told me that the school is failing in the biology classes, so let me enlighten you,' she said with us now in each other's arms having the occasional kiss, her big tits now really being felt against my chest.

'You, a male, have a penis, also known as a cock. Whereas a female has what is called a clitoris, or clit. It is their answer to the male penis and, though not very apparent, rises up to stimulation as does the male penis. Now when a person sucks on a penis, it begins to rise up into what you know as a fucking mode. Now when the female clitoris is treated the same way, it too rises up, and it is this rising up of the clitoris that excites the woman and is the forerunner in the building up to her orgasm, or cumming as in the male. Have you understood what I've said so far?' she asked. I nodded my head though I still didn't know what she was talking about not knowing about a female's clitoris. She looked at me askance, and knew that I was lost.

'Let me show you,' she then said. 'Move down the bed and get between my legs.' This I did, slithering down her sweaty body and finished up in between her legs that she had opened for me. 'Now I know you cannot see much in the darkness of the room, but use your fingers to find the opening to my sex.' This I found, running my fingers down from her pubic hairs until they were between her legs and felt the soft skin that was there. 'Now what you are touching is called the labia, the lips of my sex. Now if you push two fingers in between them, three's better, and at the top you'll find what can be called a nodule. Now this is the clitoris and just below is the entrance to the female vagina, where your cock has just been. Move one of your fingers up to this nodule and give it a rub and you will feel it start to rise up. Well maybe not now because it is already up and hard.'

This I did and she was right, for this nub of flesh was standing out and easily found by my touch, though that again is wrong for it was outside of her inside if you know what I mean.

'Now what you should do is put your thumb on my clit and use two or three fingers up inside me and move them about. Now this then excites the woman, well in most cases, into getting an orgasm, though some would rather have the male organ put inside her to bring this up to her orgasm,' she told me. Her hand then went down and gave my limp cock a rub.

'Now let's get this bugger up again and you should last a bit longer this time,' and down the bed she moved again to take the whole of my cock inside her hot mouth. I felt the foreskin being pushed down by her lips and had her tongue move over the bare flesh as she also gently chewed on me. One hand made me jump as it took hold of my balls, but then relaxed under the gentle movement of her fingers. Then she surprised me by releasing my cock only to take my balls into her mouth and I groaned at the pleasure of her sucking on them as her hand now began to massage my cock that was slowly coming to attention. After a few minutes it was once again hard as I piece of iron and she then let go of me and came back up the bed to lay on her back.

'Now, Danny. Suck on my tits and use your hand as I showed you,' she said with a smile that I could just see in the gloom of the room. This was another first for me to lower my head down to kiss the nipple of a tit before sucking on it as my hand went down to find the entrance to her pussy and put my fingers inside to do what I was told earlier. It was nice to suck on her nipple, feeling it harden up to seem almost like a nut. 'Gently nibble on it, Danny,' she said in a low voice and then gave out a moan as I did so and also felt her getting wet where my fingers were playing around inside the entrance to her vagina.

'Use the thumb to gently rub the clit while the fingers move inside. Yes, that's it. I'm on my way, Danny,' she panted, as I played with my fingers and thumb, her body giving out little flinches as she pushed my head down to be just above her pussy. So I moved further down to then start using my tongue, getting a taste of her juices that were starting to flow out of her, my first time doing this to her.

'Cunnilingus is fleeting touches with your tongue before a slow lick round it. Then make darting strikes to the vagina. Yes, yes, just like that,' she said and a few minutes later, 'Now Danny, now! Put it in and fuck me!' she cried out, and I quickly raised my head and body and moved up to lay on top of her before lifting myself up onto my elbows, feeling the head of my cock nestling itself at the entrance to her pussy and pushed my hips up and my cock slid in nice and smoothly. I could feel her inside muscles flexing themselves round my cock as I moved inside her as her legs came up over my waist, her heels then digging into my kidneys as she began to buck beneath me.

'This…is…fucking…great,' she gasped, her fingers digging into my shoulders as she was now really lifting me with her bucking. 'I'm cumming, cumming,' she cried out and I then began shooting my cum up into her, my hips ramming our pubes together and could feel some of her juices now running down my balls every time they smacked into her in their swinging back and forth as they emptied themselves.

After one big cry from her, she suddenly flopped back on the bed, her legs slipping down from my sides though she still hung onto my shoulders, and I came to a stop and found that I was breathing as heavily as she was. I felt as weak as a kitten as my arms seemed to give way and I slowly fell on top of her, squashing her nice big tits with my chest. I could feel her heart pounding away as it was being transmitted up through her tits and her hands pulled my head down and she really gave me a mashing of our lips as she kissed me.

'That's my first orgasm in nearly four years, Danny, thank you, thank you,' she said in between her kissing of me. I didn't mind this at all as it was the first woman that I had really kissed having just fucked her too. 'Peter seems to like sucking your cock, so let me try the same,' she said, trying to ease me up off of her. I lifted my upper body off and it was with some reluctance that I began to pull my still hard and erect cock out from her pussy. I could feel her trying to hold it there at the same time but it came out and the air felt cold round it after the heated oven it had just been in, and rolled over onto my back.

She was quickly up and on her side as she moved down the bed, stroking me from the chest downwards until she found my cock up on my stomach. This she grasped and lifted it upright and had her hot mouth take the head into the similar heat that it had just had a few moments before. She sucked away on it as well as using her tongue to move across the bared flesh as her hand moved the soft skin up and down the hard muscle it contained. This was heaven! Having just fucked her and now had her sucking on me. She was almost at par with Peter with her sucking, but Peter was top when it came to fucking as his place for my cock was much tighter and nicer to move my erect piece of meat in than his mother's pussy. But there again, I also liked sucking and using my tongue in her pussy, so all in all, they both are in the same level with me. Since I didn't have Peter with me, his mom was a good substitute in bed with me.

'It's been years since I did this,' she said after she had come back up the bed to kiss me, 'And I would really like to get a good taste of you later, not finding any down there just now.'

Wow! First I fuck her and now she wants me to cum in her mouth! This definitely is heaven for me.

'Go down on me again, Danny,' she said, rolling off of me, and so I kissed my way back down, taking my time to kiss and give each nipple a suck and a gently chew as she wanted me to until I was through her pubic hair, which was as soft as a mink coat, and into her pussy. On following what she had told me to do earlier, I'm pleased to say that I managed to bring her up and over the top for another orgasm. I also liked the taste of the fluids that came out of her, which was quite a lot for me to take in and swallow, nearly as good as Peter's emission of his cum.

After this, she was in my arms kissing and stroking me for quite some time until she felt I was hard again and went down and sucked on me until she got all the cum that I had inside my balls for her to taste and swallow after sucking it out of my tube.

'That tasted nice, Danny, and I think that we should do this more often,' she said after giving me a kiss and now snuggled up close to me, her arm across my chest and a tit pressed against one side. It was in this position that we fell asleep.

When I woke up, she had gone and I hadn't even felt her leaving the bed. I looked at the bedside clock and knew that George would be home by now and she was probably getting breakfast. I was quickly out of bed and showered before getting dressed and went downstairs and into the kitchen where Alice was preparing breakfast.

'Good morning, Danny,' Alice asked. 'Sleep well?'

'Good morning, Alice, yes, it's the best night I've ever had,' I smiled at her while she kept a straight face though her eyes did give out a twinkle. 'Good morning, George,' I said turning to him, sitting at the breakfast table. This meal was always had in the kitchen whereas lunch and dinner were in the dining room. 'Good night's work at the plant?'

'Boring as usual. Nothing exciting happens, except one in the past ten years,' he replied.

'What was that?' I asked. A stupid question really and knew as soon as I said it what the answer would be.

'Nearly losing my left hand,' he said with a grin as he held it up. I sat down opposite him as Alice put our two plates down in front of us before getting her own and sitting down next to him. 'What jobs you got lined up for today?' he asked of me.

'One at the Russell's place. Only a two-hour job and then back here to clean up the leaves at the bottom of the garden and mow the lawns,' I said.

'Well leave the mowing till I'm up. It's a noisy machine and I need my sleep,' he said.

'That's okay. I'll leave that till Alice goes to bed and annoy her with the noise,' I said with a grin.

'You'll do no such thing,' she cried out.

'Okay,' I said. 'I didn't want to do it in the dark anyway. Things like that are best done when you can see what you're doing,' I said with a smile on my face looking at her. She looked down at her plate, a small smile on her face and I'm sure there was a trace of a flush at my innuendo.

The rest of the meal was eaten in silence and when finished, George got up saying that it was time for his bed and said goodnight to us as I told Alice that I would wash up. I was doing this before Alice came into the kitchen after seeing that George was in his bed. Well their bed really.

'I got what you said at the table,' she hissed at me. 'Don't do it again. You might go too far one day.' I was drying my hands as she spoke and now I took her into my arms and gave her a good kiss which she didn't stop me from doing.

'Thank you for last night. It was wonderful,' I said, holding her to my chest, feeling her breasts being pressed against me.

'Yes it was, but as I've just said. Be careful what you say in front of George for if he finds out. One-handed or not, he'd kill the pair of us,' she said, giving me a kiss on the nose. 'Now off you go to the Russell's and I'll see you back here at lunch time.'

Off I went to fix a leak under the sink, and with a lot of plumbing jobs, the hose and fittings were now of plastic and I could have done the job in an hour and a half, but dragged it out to the two hours that I'd said. On getting paid after I'd finished, I gave them a receipt, something I was meticulous about as I would have to pay taxes at the end of the year and also, for some people, it was needed for their insurance company.

There was one insurance company, that after checking some claims and seeing my work, now began to ask me to do repairs in my locality on their behalf, so I was also getting work from them now, which was good in terms of payment.

One job I had that wasn't related to any insurance company, was a good one for me. It was at the Steiner's house and they were thinking of having the loft converted, but wanted a dormer window put in first to see if having this conversion would be worthwhile. If I did a good job with the window then they would decide on the conversion and I would get the job. Now their son, Ralph, had been at the same high school I went to and was three years older than me, but the word was that he was gay, and it looked as though by his mannerisms and the like. I found out that it was a fact.

It had been damn well hot in that loft and I had stripped down to wearing just boots and a pair of shorts. Also, the place was full of dust. It was nice to have gotten through the roof to get some air in there and began the real work of fixing the frame into the hole. Ralph came up several times to see how I was getting on and bringing me up cold drinks for he saw that I was really sweating up there and getting covered in dust that stuck to me.

On his final visit to the loft, he had changed into sand shoes and shorts and even helped me clear up the mess that I had made and finished up as dirty as I was. He was pleased with the work I had done and said so and suggested that now that it was finished that we both could do with a shower. We exited the loft and he led me to his bedroom that had an en-suite bathroom and it was here that we went.

'The shower's big enough for the pair of us to wash at the same time,' he said, stripping off his shoes and shorts to get inside and turn on the water. Recalling what had been said at school about him, I guessed that this might be the come on to be naked with him in the shower. I shrugged my shoulders and took off my boots and shorts not minding if he wanted sex for hadn't I with Peter? So as naked as he was, got into the shower with him. He looked at my cock that was semi hard at the earlier thoughts as I looked at his which wasn't as big as mine.

'That's a nice looking cock you've got, Danny,' he said, soaping up a flannel. 'Turn round and let me wash your back,' which I did. 'And a nice pair of plums too,' as he washed my back, spending more on the cheeks of my bum than my back. 'Okay, back done, now the front,' he said and I turned to face him to see the smile on his face as he soaped the flannel again and began on my chest and worked his way down to start on my cock and balls which were not really dirty, but got washed all the same. Of course, with his hand now being used instead of the flannel, as he washed me, he was virtually masturbating me with his hand movements. Well you can guess the result of this and you are right, for it rose up to be hard and sticking out in front of me while he was washing it.

'That's a lovely cock you've got, Danny. Can I suck on it? He asked me as he rinsed the soap off of it.

'Be my guest,' I replied, leaning back against the tiled wall as he went down onto his knees and took the head of my cock inside his hot mouth. He didn't seem to mind the water cascading down on his head as he began to suck me, giving me a quick look as he tongued me at the same time. I gave out a groan at the pleasure he was giving me, being an expert at fellatio. So much so that he was able to take the whole length of my cock into his mouth and into his throat, his nose buried in my pubic hairs. By not having to hold the shaft as he sucked, he was able to bring both hands round to the cheeks of my bum that he caressed as he sucked.

'I'm cumming,' I said with grunts as I began to push myself towards his face, now moving his head back so that he only had the head in there, his lips clamped tight round the base of it as I began giving him my cum to taste before swallowing. Which, being the pro at this that he was, he took it all in first to collect it together and be moved round in his mouth before swallowing it all in one go.

'Lovely,' he said, taking his head up off me briefly to speak before taking it back inside to finish the job. He looked up grinning at me, still ignoring the water splashing all over his face and came up from off of his knees and gently gave each nipple on my chest a nibble before coming up to hold my body against his, his hands sliding up from my bum cheeks to hold my back as he kissed me. 'You sure had a lot of cum there, and it was lovely. Pure nectar,' he said after breaking off the kiss.

'You were great, Ralph. That's the best head anyone has given me,' I said, my arms now round his back in the same hold as he had me.

'Have you had many?' he asked.

'No,' I said, 'but you are far and above those that have given me head.'

'We should do this again then. I'll tell dad that you've done a wonderful job on fitting the window into the roof, and I will not be telling lies because it's perfect. Then you'll get the job of turning the loft into whatever it is that dad wants and I will help you do the work. You won't have to pay me in cash, for all that I would want in payment would be for you to fuck me with this lovely tool you've got.' This last being said as he had taken hold of my still hard erection. 'Would you?'

'I can't think of any other way but as you have suggested,' I said smiling back at him.

'Lovely,' he said and kissed me again.

So that was the start of me then having not only a helper in doing this loft conversion, but got to fuck him every afternoon during the time it took to do the job that his father was paying me for.

It took 10 days to turn that loft into a lovely extra-large room adding another window in the roof, electricity, the walls and finishing up with carpeting the whole floor. I then did another four days in putting up a solid staircase as means of access instead of the ladder that had been used before. Even if I say so myself, it was a grand looking place when I'd finished, much to the disappointment of Ralph since completing the job means not having me in the house every day to fuck.

The more I worked, the stronger I became physically, what with lifting bags of cement and heavy wooden parts. I even put a bit more weight on, though not a lot to be gross. Now being six foot in height and weighing in at around a hundred-and-forty pounds, really muscled arms and thighs, and even my cock seemed to have grown with the rest of my body by being just over seven inches erect and having quite a wide girth that I haven't as yet measured. I'm good looking and still don't need to shave and have a hairless chest though my forearms and legs had some but not the matted sort.

I think it was more my physique than my work that attracted older women and some men towards me with the aim of having sex, many of which I accepted. For a woman, I would go down and suck a pussy before fucking her, while man will go down on me and then fuck him too. It was grand and I was enjoying life as I approached 19.

Having spent my two hours at the Russell's house, I returned to Peter's to be greeted with a smile from Alice, who gave me a light lunch of mostly salad, washed down with a beer before starting to work at the far end of the garden where there were a lot of trees that always seemed to be shedding their leaves. These I had been racking up and putting into a wheelbarrow to take to the small incinerator that was behind our workshop.

It was late afternoon that Alice brought me down a can of a cold fruit juice that was most welcome, and as I drank it, she ran her hand down my arm, feeling the sweat that had collected there, then surprised me by giving the arm a lick.

'I like the smell of a working man,' she said, moving in closer to me and taking me into her arms and giving me a kiss. I wasn't wearing a shirt and now had her body pressed up tight to mine, and after the lick of my arm, the kiss and now her body tight to mine, my body reacted and I got a hard on inside my shorts. We were out of sight of the house and had her hips move themselves sideways, aggravating my already hard cock.

'Nobody can see us,' she whispered into my mouth and went down onto her knees, pulling my shorts down as she did so, making my cock spring up as it was uncovered and had her take the head into her mouth to start sucking on. There was nothing I could, or want to really, but gave out a groan and took hold of her head into my hands to face fuck her. Sweat was still rolling down my back and felt it moving down the crack between the cheeks of my bum, but couldn't move from the pleasure I was getting as she sucked and teased the bare flesh of the head of my cock and then got the whole load of my cum shooting out in a never ending stream to fill her mouth.

I felt the head being compressed as she swallowed it all, one hand still moving on my shaft, trying to get any more out of me while the other hand was running up and down my left leg until she released me and stood up and kissed me with her wet lips.

'That was lovely, Danny. Let's hope you build up the same amount by bedtime,' she said, giving me kiss on the nose and picking up the empty can that I had dropped, went off back to the house. Bemused, I pulled up my shorts and carried on clearing the ground round the trees, making a good job of it for I wouldn't be mowing the lawns until George was up from his bed.

Judging by the sun that filtered through the trees, guessed it was close to dinner time and packed away the wheelbarrow and raked and made sure that the incinerator was okay before going into the house and upstairs for a shower. I was now almost a resident in Peter's house with me sleeping over six nights a week now, it was only on a Monday night that I slept in my own home, the night that George wasn't on duty at the plant. I had lots of my clothes in the bedroom in various places and so after my shower, making sure that my cock was really clean, got dressed and went down to have dinner with George and Alice.

'Well I didn't hear the lawnmower going, Danny,' George said as we ate.

'That's because I haven't started on that yet, but will after this lovely dinner. Thank you, Alice,' I said, giving her a smile and licked my lips and she got the message that it was also for the afternoon blow job. Then with the meal over, I excused myself saying that I was off to start doing the mowing of the lawns and heard George speak to Alice after he thought I was out of earshot.

'He's almost a resident here now, Alice,' he'd said.

'Well that's okay with me for he's doing all those things that need doing that you can't do now, George,' she'd replied, and that's all I caught and wondered if that last remark had anything to do with sex. For that, he should still be capable.

I got changed into some working gear and went out and started cutting the grass. I later heard the car leave with George but carried on till it began to get dark, that was when I packed up having done nearly half of the grass that needed cutting. I had a choice of beer or coffee when I entered the house via the kitchen and opted for the coffee not wanting the alcohol if I was going to have a repeat of the last night.

'Well, I'm off to bed…….' I began but didn't finish what I wanted to say, hoping that she would pick up where I had left off.

'It's rather early, but, well, I'll follow you as soon as I've tidied up a bit,' she said, which was enough for me and went up to the room I slept in and undressed and had a shower before getting into bed. Well on it really, having pushed the covering sheet down so that I was then completely naked on it. I didn't turn off the bedside lamp but left it on for if she did come into bed with me, I wanted to be able to see her nakedness and what I had to play with. She knew what she had to play with at having seen it, felt it and even tasted it out in the garden that afternoon.

It must have been half an hour after I got on the bed that she came into the room, wearing a dressing gown and came and stood by the bed looking down at me lying there, with a raging hard on that lay up on my stomach.

'Did you know that it covers your navel when it's lying there like that?' she said still looking at my cock lying there.

'No,' I replied and put my hand down and found that the head did indeed cover it which made it at least seven inches long if not more, never having given any thought to what the length was before.

'It's even past the sun tan line that you've got round the waist,' she said as she shrugged the robe off of her shoulders and let it slide down onto the carpet, showing me her full length nakedness. Her tits were big, nice and firm for a woman of her age and are the two items that I liked kissing, especially the nipples, making them rise up to hard little nodules. 'Move over,' she said as she began to get on the bed with me. I moved over and had her roll onto her side, pressing a tit against my chest as she kissed me.

It was lovely to have her lying half over me as we kissed. Loving her as much as I did Peter and even more when she moved down the bed to take my erection into her mouth. But she then went and changed her position on the bed not letting go of my cock from her mouth, turning around on her knees, feeling her tits brush across my lower chest as she straddled me and had her pussy just above my face. I brought my hands up and had her sit on the palms as she lowered her pussy down to my mouth for me to start pleasing her with my tongue as she was doing to me.

With the bedside lamp on, I could now really see what a women's sex looked like and must say that it isn't the most wonderful sight in the world, but once your tongue was doing its job in there, you couldn't see it anymore. I did note that her clit stood out at the top above the urethra where she pissed from and below this the entrance to her vagina. As she often gave the head of my cock a squeeze, making the eye of my cock open for her to poke it with her tongue, I had no compunction about tonguing her urethra. That was after rasping her clit and before plunging my tongue into her vagina.

Playing with her clit was the means of exciting her so that her body would start to build up to her orgasm, much the same as she was doing to the head of my cock and the G-spot. Mind you, her hand was active during my arousal by rubbing the shaft and giving it a squeeze from time to time.

With some of her juices now beginning to come down into my mouth, I knew that she was getting close to her orgasm and really had to fight my own body to hold back my emission until she let go of hers. With her grinding her pussy down as hard as she could to me, her body started to shake and boy, didn't she squirm and give out a low cry as she flooded my mouth with her cum and then I let go of mine to do the same to her. She was then bouncing up and down on my face as my hips were bucking up to hers as we both gave our all into each other's mouths.

It's easier in cleaning up a cock afterwards that it is with a pussy, for some fluid still came out of her whereas my cumming was finished after the last shot, but it satisfied her enough for me to carrying on licking her out until she pulled herself off of me at both ends. I could now breathe properly and took in quite a quantity of air into my lungs as she turned back round on the bed and lay atop of me. Her breasts, with the now hard nipples trying to push themselves into my chest as the whole pair got squashed as she kissed me, getting a taste of her own juices that still coated my lips and chin.

'As much as this afternoon and just as lovely, Danny,' she breathed, 'plus an orgasm for me this time. I can hardly wait until you're ready again and have you inside me.'

'The same goes for me too, Alice,' I replied, rolling her over to her back and began a downward excursion, lingering at each nipple to make them rise up again to be hard nuts on top of their mounds. My fingers too were busy inside her pussy, getting her nice and wet before I went right down and began sucking and licking at the insides of her body. I must be getting better at this for it wasn't long before she had her second orgasm which I lapped up and carried on playing with her pussy until my cock was back up in its fighting mode.

I moved back up her body and she gave out a little cry as she felt the head of my erection probing the entrance to her sex and her legs came up and I smoothly slid inside that heated interior.

'Lovely cowboy,' she said when I was fully inside her, feeling her muscles playing all alongside my shaft, making it twitch as it throbbed in the heat that was there. 'Ride and fuck me senseless, you stud of a man.' This I did and brought pleasure to both of us when she had another orgasm with me cumming inside her at the same time. We had fun afterwards at licking each other clean before we cuddled together before falling asleep.

Like the previous morning, she was gone when I woke up, probably having gone back to her own bed to muss it up before George went there after breakfast. That became our pattern every night, except Mondays when I slept at my own home turning up for dinner.

'Hello, stranger,' dad said to me as I sat down with my brothers and sisters at the dining table. 'Long time, no see.'

'I was here last week,' I countered.

'Why do you sleep over there every night of the week?' he asked and mom got in first with the answer.

'That's Alice's idea, Robert,' mom told my dad. 'With George now working nights, she doesn't like cooking her meals to eat alone, plus she feels safer having a man sleeping there at nights.' Dad made a rude noise with his nose at this.

'There's no need to snort. I wouldn't like to sleep alone in the house at night,' she said.

'Does she sleep alone?' dad asked with a smirk on his face as he looked at me.

'She has her bed and I have mine,' I replied, keeping a straight face and not blushing. 'Besides, she's as good a cook as mom. With George being off on a Monday means she's not alone and so I can sleep here.' I could have said more but kept it short for the least said, etc. Then it was dropped with my siblings wanting to put their oar in and speaking of what they wanted to say about other things. It was lonely in my bed those Monday nights.

The next day, Tuesday, could have been a disaster for me, but it turned out well in the end. I had a job at the Carlow's house where some tiles had come off the roof and had damaged the gutter and I was to replace the tiles firmly and see what I could do with the guttering. It was at the back where they had a big lovely swimming pool, so I had to make sure that the ladder wouldn't slip on the tiles. That was the easy part. As both Mr. and Mrs. Carlow worked, the house would be empty though I was told to help myself with food and drinks from the fridge for my lunch, for which I thanked her, and I was told that I could have a swim when I'd finished if I wanted to. I thanked her again and she went off to work, her husband having already left.

So I replaced the tiles making sure they were firmly attached and the guttering wasn't a problem for it hadn't been broken, only having come adrift from its brackets so that was soon done. It was still early afternoon when I'd finished and having put the ladder back in their shed, looked longingly at the pool with its shimmering water in the sun and decided to have a swim.

Now I didn't have a swimming costume with me but with everything quiet all around, thought that it would be alright to have my swim without wearing one. So I took my clothes off in the kitchen and got a big towel from one of the bathrooms and went out to the pool. I looked around to see if anybody was about, but didn't see anyone and it was all very quiet except for a few birds chattering away. So off came the towel and into that lovely cool water I dived.

It was lovely swimming up and down without wearing a costume, being bollock naked and loving the feel of the water flowing past my bared cock and balls. Twenty minutes was enough to rid me of the sweat that I'd had from working in the sun, and climbed out of the pool, not bothering to use the steps at the shallow end, and dried myself and wrapped the towel around my waist and went back into the house to get a drink from the fridge.

The kitchen faced the pool and I stood by the sink looking out when I saw two young kids wandering around the pool. Now where in hell did they come from, was my first thought and then noticed that a side gate to the next door's property was open, so that then was the answer. They were both about five years old and one was a girl and one a boy, being able to tell the difference because one had long hair and the other short. They just wore a small pair of shorts and were barefoot as they walked round the pool, eyeing the water, no doubt wishing they could swim in their neighbor's pool.

It was no business of mine so I wasn't going to say anything until it happened. The girl had reached the place where I had got out of the pool and it was there that the tiles were wet and the girl skidded in this and fell over and into the pool. Now I knew it was deep at this part of the pool and so I dropped my can of drink in the sink and rushed out to see her going under the water and I dived in.

Now with the speed that I hit the water, it tore the towel from around my waist, though I didn't notice this at the time, concentrating on just getting that girl out of the pool before she drowned. She was below the surface when I reached her and lifted her out and backpedalled to the side and then heaved her out onto the tiles and climbed out myself. I started to panic for she wasn't moving and I quickly put my hands together and started to press down on her bare chest, having water then pumping out of her mouth. I did this several times until no more water came out and then started what they call the Kiss of Life. Breathing heavily into her open mouth between pumping her chest.

Her brother, well I assumed he was, was standing nearby crying his eyes out as I was trying to resuscitate the girl, pump with the hands, breath in to her mouth, pump the chest again. That's when a big foot collided with my head, knocking me almost senseless as I fell over onto my back.

'Pervert!' I heard being shouted, though it seemed to be coming from way off as I had another heavy kick catch me just below my ribs at the waist. This blew the air out of me and I lay there gasping for air and it took a few minutes before I was able to move and roll on my side to see people round the girl who was now being sat up and having her back pounded.

I saw that the people were a man kneeling down by the girl, two older women and two teenage girls were standing there watching the girl now coughing and thank heaven, starting to breathe again. But then I noticed that one of the women and the two girls were not looking at the girl but at me, though they were not looking at my face but at my body. It was then that I realised that I was there by the poolside, naked and letting them see all that I had.

I struggled to my feet, my head still ringing and a pain on my side as I staggered a little to get myself upright and looked in the pool to see my towel submerged in the water. I didn't hesitate to jump in and grab hold of it and swam to the shallow end and had to struggle to get the heavy towel wrapped round my waist before getting up the steps to walk around where they were now crowding around the girl. They were also listening to the little boy who was evidently telling them what had happened.

'Is she alright?' I asked them, leaning over slightly, holding my side where I'd been kicked.

'Yes,' said the man, getting up and facing me. 'I apologise most profusely for kicking you for my mind jumped to the wrong conclusion upon seeing you naked and kissing my daughter. It was just an instinct that I lashed out and I am most humbly sorry that I misread what you were doing. Thank you for saving her from drowning. If there's anything I can do to make amends for my error, say the word.' I must say, that his apology was uttered with all sincerity and with a contrite look on his face.

'I'm glad she's okay. I was in the kitchen when I saw her fall in and had no other thought in my mind except to get her out of the pool as quick as I could. That my towel came off in the water, I didn't realise this for I was more concerned at getting the water out of her lungs and get breath back into her body,' I replied.

'Well it was a courageous act,' one of the women said, guessing that she was the mother, 'And I heartily thank you for your prompt action.' She then came over and kissed me. 'I think you've pleased the girls too,' she whispered before letting go of me. I'm sure I blushed now as I looked at the girls, seeing them smile back at me, eyes dropping to look at the towel round my waist.

'Well I'm sorry that I exhibited myself before them. It wasn't intentional' I told the woman.

'Don't worry about that for at their age, I think they would have seen a man naked before, but there again, maybe not as well-endowed as you are,' she finished with a big smile on her face that made me blush even more.

'Well the girl's in safe hands now, so I'd better be going,' I said and quickly moved off before any more was said, getting back into the house and finding another towel to dry myself and hanging the wet one up on the shower curtain rail above the bath. When dry, I went back to the kitchen and got dressed, looking out of the window and saw that they had all gone and that the gate that the two kids had used to enter the garden, was now closed.

I went off home, well not mine, but to Peter's house, the pain in my side now having very much diminished and gave no more thought to what I had done. It was something that any other person, man or woman would have done in saving a child from drowning. Though I did have to think of it again when I turned up to meet Alice in the kitchen. She greeted me with a kiss then stood back and looked closer to my face.

'What happened? You got a big bruise coming up on your cheek,' she said, pushing me down onto a chair and going out for a moment or two and coming back with a bottle of witch hazel. This she poured out onto a tissue and began wiping over the bruise that I didn't know I had. So I gave her a short version of what had happened and had her kiss me again calling me a hero.

I thought that it was all over but found out the next day that the girl's father had taken a step further regarding the event. Of course I had the usual sex that night with Alice, with her constantly calling me a hero until I told her finally to shut up and the best way of doing this was to stick my prick in her mouth.

But after breakfast with her and George, I went out into the back garden to finish off clearing up the dead leaves and was just coming up to lunch when Alice called out and as I came out of the trees wearing just my boots and shorts, saw that she had a woman and a man with her. The man carrying a camera who immediately started taking pictures of me as they got closer.

'This lady and gentleman are from the local Tribune and have come to see you,' Alice said, a big smile on her face. So the father of the child I had saved had gone to the local newspaper to tell them how I had saved his daughter from drowning. So I had to tell them what happened, her taking notes as the guy took more pictures of me. I was glad when they left and had Alice cling to my arm and taking me back into the house.

She pulled me into the parlor and to my surprise, pulled off her dress to show that she was naked beneath and quickly pulled my shorts down, pushing me back onto the sofa to take my boots off too. Just seeing her naked there before me made me start to rise up and by the time she got my boots off, I was up as hard as an iron bar and had her give the head a quick suck before she pulled me off the sofa to land on her as she lay back on the carpet.

'Fuck me, lover. It turned me on when it was thought that you were trying to have sex with a little girl, being naked there above her. Fuck me, Danny, and give me what's mine and not theirs,' she panted with this enigmatic ending to what she had just said. What's mine? Not theirs? My cock was not just for her but Peter too. Theirs? Was she referring to the two young girls that were there? She was when I saw later what the newspaper had printed, obviously having been told by the reporter what the girls had said.

But she was there on the carpet with her legs open. My cock was throbbing away fit to bust. She wanted it and I wanted her and so as I fell on top of her, my cock found its own way up inside her and brought her to two orgasms before I gave her my cum.

With the Tribune being a local paper, it was only issued every Thursday and Alice made sure that she had three copies delivered that morning. On the front page was a picture of me, covered in sweat and only wearing my shorts and boots in the garden. "Reluctant Hero Saves Drowning Girl" was the headline, and a brief couple of lines before you had to go further into the paper for the rest. As you know what happened, I'll only tell you the odd bits that I didn't know at the time. "Anna, the five year old daughter of Angus McAndrew, co-owner of this newspaper, had his daughter saved from drowning by young Danny Rundene." It went on with what you know but with a comment from the two girls there that they were proud of the young man who, naked, had saved the girl and he was a big man in all senses of the word. This latter was in brackets.

'I bet you could bed both those girls at the drop of your shorts,' Alice chuckled as she read this out to me, before carrying on to the end of the article.

Mom, at home, had been inundated with phone calls from many people that she knew, talking about what they had read in the paper, saying that she should be proud of her son in his heroic act, well most of them were along those lines, she told me on the following Monday. That's not all on that day, for we also had a visitor.

The knock at the door was seen to by mom just after breakfast and just before I went off to one of my jobs. The visitor was none other than the co-owner of the newspaper, Angus McAndrew himself.

'Hello, Danny,' he said, shaking my hand after being invited into the house. 'I've come to apologise again for attacking you when you were trying to save my daughter, for which I much regret at jumping to the wrong conclusion. I had your heroic deed put out which no doubt you have seen and I have done some checking up on you. Your name is quite familiar with a lot of people around here and not one had a bad word to say about you. That you were a good worker and helped many people save money by working well under the going rates on whatever job you undertook.' Mom was standing a little behind him, smiling away at what he was saying.

'So in a way of saying thank you again for saving Anna's life, I'm giving you something that will help you in the good work you are doing here in this locality. Here,' and he took me by the arm and lead me back to the front door and on opening it, pointed to a small pick-up truck that was parked on the drive.

'That's for you with me and the wife's heartfelt thanks,' and he gave me the keys to this brand new vehicle. 'Better start taking driving lessons,' he chuckled. With that, he said his goodbyes to me and mom, the rest of my siblings looking on in awe, and left to get into his own car that had a driver to return to his newspaper.

To finish off this little escapade, dad was pleased with what I had been given and he had, in the past, been taking us boys out for driving lessons in his car. So within a month, I took my driving test and passed and so I was legally allowed to drive my very own pickup truck to carry my tools and any materials that I needed in my work. The papers in the truck had been made out in my name with a full year's insurance too.

I later did get to bed one of those girls that were there by the pool that day.

I was surprised at the number of small jobs that Alice kept finding for me to do in between the work I was getting more often with my name being bantered around town. It was one afternoon having no outside work to do that she pulled me into the workshop that Peter and I had built.

'You've had sex with Peter in here, now it's my turn,' she said, stripping off her dress and spreading herself out on the sofa where she had seen Peter and myself having sex. My clothes were off in a flash and was soon coupled with her on that same sofa, bringing her up to an orgasm and me cumming inside her at the same time. I got the usual cry from her when I pulled out but had no objections to lying back and having her straddle me afterwards so that she could suck on my still hard cock while I suck her pussy.

After which, we lay together on the sofa, kissing and stroking each other's body, quite content with the sexual relationship we had together.

'Peter will be home next week from the university,' she said, and I could see some tears in her eyes. 'I'm going to miss being in bed with you when he does, knowing that the two of you will be sleeping and having sex together and me sleeping alone. I'm already feeling jealous at what I'll be missing and at what he will be getting instead of me. I love you, Danny,' she said, the latter being almost a whisper.

'I love you too, Alice, and I also love Peter and cannot say anything otherwise. I also love George, but that's only because he's away at night for us to make love together. Even though I love Peter. Love having sex with him, I also love having sex with you. It's a cross we'll have to bear as under no circumstances do I want to break up a family by loving both of you.' I had to sniff as I felt tears in my eyes at her declaration of love for me, but I had said the truth in the fact that I loved both of them and wouldn't want to choose between them.

'It might be wrong for me to say this, but you can, if you feel inclined, always come and watch us sometime when Peter and I are here on this sofa and imagine that it's you that I'm fucking,' I said to her.

'Then tonight you can fuck me in the doggie position so that I can picture myself being fucked when you fuck him,' she said.

'What about when he's fucking me?' I asked. 'You can't do the same to me,' and it made her chuckle.

'I could if you'd like a dildo up your ass,' and she carried on with her chuckle at the thought, one that I shook my head about and said no to. 'Why not?' she asked.

'If Peter fucks me bare back, I can then have the thrill of feeling his cum shoot in to coat my channel. You can't do that with the fake prick of a dildo,' I answered back.

'If only I was an hermaphrodite, then I could have it both ways,' she sighed.

So for the rest of the time before Peter would be home, we fucked at every opportunity that we could manage during the day with George being in bed asleep and at night when he was at the plant. I never gave it a thought that I was cuckolding him by fucking his wife. I felt sorry for her as she was the one who would be missing out over the six weeks that Peter would be home. But then I had to look at Peter's side of it, for he had been away for nearly twelve weeks now and had missed out on being with me. Did he find another lover at the university? That was something that I didn't want to know about even if he did. I'd rather Peter tell me a lie and that he had stayed true to me and this then brought on a great feeling of guilt that I hadn't saved myself up for him. Oh what a fucking tangled web I had gotten myself into.

Alice and I were on tenterhooks on Sunday, for Peter had left the university the day before and was due home this day. Alice and I had fucked away most of the Saturday night, what with it being our last night together for the next six weeks and boy, didn't we look tired and drawn the next morning at breakfast. Even George noticed how Alice looked and remarked on it, but she said that knowing that Peter was due home this day that she hardly got a wink of sleep. How I managed to keep a straight face, I don't know.

She had worked hard cleaning the house and his room the day before and now everything was ready for him to come home, home to his house and me. George was up earlier than normal, for he wanted to pick

Peter up in his car at the bus station and duly went off with us knowing the time he was expected to arrive.

With Alice and myself left alone, she took me into her arms and kissed me fiercely. 'Now don't breathe a word about us being together at nights,' she said.

'I wouldn't dream of it!' I replied, somewhat shocked at her saying this, for there's no way would I have mentioned that I'd been fucking his mother whilst he was away. I got another kiss like the last one before she broke away and went off to the kitchen to start preparing his favourite dinner.

We were both out on the drive when the car arrived and Peter was quickly out of the car and into the arms of Alice to be kissed by her as she hugged him. He then came over to me and gave me a hug, but no kisses for his parents were both watching this male greeting.

'I've missed you all so much,' he cried, 'and I'm glad to be home.' I went and took Peter's bag from George who had got it out of the trunk, and took it upstairs to his room as he talked to his parents in the parlor. He was telling them how good it was at the university though the food there wasn't a patch on his mother's cooking.

I saw to laying out the table in the dining room while George, a bit awkwardly with his gammy hand, opened up some wine bottles to celebrate Peter's arrival. The meal was excellent and he didn't stop talking the whole time and even carried on afterwards until late in the evening.

'Are you staying over?' he asked of me giving me a shy smile.

'Of course, Peter. I couldn't miss this homecoming,' I replied.

'And a lovely homecoming it was too,' he said to his parents. 'Thank you. But I'm off to bed now. It's been a tiring and a long day. Goodnight all.'

We said our goodnights and he went off to bed.

'I'm turning in too,' I said, 'For I've got work to do tomorrow and not have the day off like George.'

'I like that!' he exclaimed. 'I'm just about to go off to work now while you can sleep.' With that, he gave Alice a kiss and I left them to go up to the room I normally slept in. Here, I undressed and had a shower and cleaned my teeth and waited for Alice to go to her room before leaving mine to go to Peter's. I heard her knock on Peter's door and say a few words to him that I didn't catch and then heard his door being shut as she went off to her room. I think she made a point of shutting her door with some force so that I could hear it and know that it was clear for me to leave my room.

I closed my door quietly and that of Peter's when I entered his room. The bedside lamp was on and he was sitting up in bed, waiting for me. I had on a dressing gown and quickly shook this off for Peter to see my naked body with my erection sticking out in front of me in the anticipation of him having it.

He had a big smile on his face and threw back the sheet that had covered him to show that he too had an erection and opened his arms for me to fall into as I climbed on the bed to be hugged. Not only hugged, but kissed with some fervour.

'Oh Danny. You don't know how much I have been dreaming of this moment,' he said as I lay on top of him, our erect cocks being squashed together against our stomachs. We kissed and let our tongues play with each other as our bodies moved to feel the hard cocks that we had.

'I've missed you so much. Not having you in bed with me at nights and having to jerk myself off wishing that it was you doing it and then fucking me with your lovely cock. Fuck me now,' he whispered in my ear. 'I've been wanting it for so long. Use a condom so that I can suck you afterwards.' I gave him a grin and rolled off and got a condom out of the bedside table drawer where he kept them. A stupid place to keep them for Alice surely knew they were there having cleaned his room, but then she knew we fucked each other so it wasn't really a problem.

With the condom pulled out of its wrapper, I was up on my knees to roll it down over my cock as Peter watched me doing this, licking his lips knowing that he would be sucking on it after I had cum inside him. With it in place, he rolled over onto his front and rose up onto his knees, presenting me with his ass that he wanted me to fuck.

This I did, sliding my covered cock into that tight hole of his, loving the feel of his muscle flexing itself round the shaft as I entered to fill him with my throbbing hard cock.

'Fucking lovely, Danny,' he crooned as I filled him. Holding his hips in a firm grip until I was buried inside up to the hilt. I was back in my other heaven which was better than a woman's pussy. For a moment, I savoured the heat of his internal body and having him in this position with my cock pulsating away before I began to slowly fuck his lovely tight ass.

'Harder, Danny,' he grunted. 'Harder and faster. Really give it to me.' So I upped my pace and began ramming my cock into him, my balls slapping the lower cheeks of his bum as I did so. This aggravated the semen in them and soon wanted their release, and pulling him back to me as I rammed forward, I felt my cum rising up and held him tight as I began pumping the cum out into his ass.

'I can feel you cumming,' he cried out in a low voice, moving himself back onto me at every forward thrust until I had given him all that I had. I found I was panting heavily and leaned over his rear end as I came to a stop, and also felt sweat on my forehead, the odd bead dropping down onto his back. 'Lovely,' he crooned, his muscle flexing like mad to try and squeeze more cum out of the shaft that was still throbbing away inside him. 'Noooo,' he cried as I pulled out, his muscle trying to stop me leaving his ass, but it came out and I sat back on my heels as he quickly turned round and pulled the condom off of me and took the head of my wet cock into his mouth.

'Mmmm,' he mumbled between slurps as he sucked any cum that was there, out of me as well as the coating over the head. He also gently chewed it as he sucked and kept giving out little sighs as he cleaned up my still hard cock until he was done. He released me and gave the head a final kiss before rising up and giving me a taste of my own cum as he kissed me.

'My favourite one and only lover,' he panted between our kissing. 'I loved that and can't wait to have it again.' With me having risen up onto my knees now had both our cocks being pressed together between us and I now wanted his cock inside me

'Your turn now to give me what I've been missing also, Peter,' I said, breaking up the hugging and kissing. He grinned at me and moved over to get another condom out while I then fell forward onto my knees and rested my upper body on my lower arms with my ass up in the air for him to now fuck me.

I didn't get a chance to give his cock a suck before he had it on and was behind me, hands on my hips and making my body quiver at feeling the head of his cock probe the entrance to my backside. Oh what bliss it was to feel him expanding me and having his throbbing cock once again enter to give me a thrill. I think that we were both crooning away in time to his movements, both of us having the pleasure, him from fucking me and me in being fucked.

But such was his need, there was no need for me to tell him to push harder and faster, for he was doing it anyway while he was holding my hips firmly as he pulled me back onto his forward thrusts as he shot his load up into the condom. Like me, his exertions seemed to drain him of strength, for he fell full length onto me, bearing me down onto the bed with him still throbbing away inside me. It had been many weeks since he'd been inside me, so I just loved having him where he was now, loving his weight and lovely cock still inside me. I loved Peter enough to keep on using the superlative to describe my feelings and what I felt with him both on top and inside me once again.

I too gave out that little cry at losing that pulsating organ inside me and was quick to roll over and scrabble my way to see his grinning face as I stripped off the condom to take his lovely cock once again into my mouth to suck out any excess cum. I just loved having his cock again where it was as I sucked and chewed on it until the head was clean of his cum.

I let go of him and rose up for us to hold each other in an embrace as we kissed and rolled over to lay on the bed as we told each other of our love. Needless to say that we fucked each other again a little while later but after that, he soon fell asleep in my arms after such a long day for him and it wasn't long before I too fell asleep.

So once again there were four of us at the breakfast table, Peter answering all the questions about his university asked by both his mom and dad. Though the place was called an Arts and Craft University, he had opted for the designs section, narrowing the field down to things mechanical. Like motors, for boats, cars and bikes, tractors, diggers and things like that, adding aircraft too, though this was a separate one and even harder than the rest. But he was knuckling down to find out which suited him best to concentrate on.

Alice had already asked how he had slept in his own bed again, and smiled at his answer that it was his best night since he had left home. I soon had to go off to a job I had lined up, leaving them still talking and didn't return until the late afternoon.

In the kitchen I found Alice on her own preparing things for dinner.

'Where's Peter?' I asked, guessing that George was still in bed.

'In the workshop. Waiting for you, I think,' she said with a smile.

'How long have we got?' I asked, knowing she would know to what I was referring to.

'Let's say about an hour,' was the answer.

'Will you be taking a peek?' I smiled at her.

'I might. Just to see what you are up to,' she answered.

'You know damn well what we'll be up to. He's been without it for so long I bet he's clock watching. See you later,' I said before leaving the kitchen and going out and on to the workshop.

I barely got inside the door before he was in my arms, kissing me and dragging me to the sofa.

'It's been a long day waiting for you to come home,' he said, already getting my shirt off, which didn't take long, nor getting the rest of my clothes. His clothes were already down on his knees and so I sucked the erection that had quickly risen up knowing what he wanted.

'Dinner's in less than an hour, Peter,' I said, pulling myself out of his mouth. 'Let's make the most of it.' He was quickly onto the sofa on his knees and my cock had enough of his saliva on it as a lubricant and I quickly got behind and shoved my throbbing cock up into his ass.

'Heavenly,' he gurgled as I fucked him and wondered if Alice was watching me fuck her son. It wasn't long before I gave him my cum and after pulling out and wiping my cock on some cloth, went onto my knees and had him fuck me. There was no sucking of cocks after going bare back and so got dressed and went off to the house.

'I think you both need a shower before dinner,' Alice said as we entered the kitchen. 'You look all sweaty.' Which was a fact and so we went and had our shower, not together, just in case she came upstairs and I was dressed and back down before Peter.

'Did you get a look in?' I asked her in a low voice, us being the only two there.

'Yes, and it turned me on and wished that it was me on my knees on the sofa,' she replied, which was all we could say for both Peter and George had come into the kitchen.

It was a lovely six weeks of fucking Peter every afternoon and twice at night and having the same done to me. There was only one time that Alice and I could have sex together and that was one of the Mondays. George was on his day off and had taken Peter out in the car to give him driving lessons leaving Alice and myself alone. I had taken the afternoon off knowing what Peter would be doing and so, just after they had left, Alice almost dragged me up to the room I slept in and we were quickly naked on the bed to kiss and fondle each other. She loved me sucking her pussy and with the use of fingers and thumb as well as my tongue, brought her up to an orgasm and then gave her another one when I fucked her. It was nice to have her once again sucking on my cock after having pulled out of her, and overall, it was a lovely afternoon, but the only one we had during those six weeks.

Peter's last night was agony for both of us, with him crying and making me cry too as we kissed and fondled each other both before and after having sex. Both trying to give the other the best we could do in both the oral and anal sex we had in bed on that last night. Neither of us slept with us fucking and sucking each other off three times and we looked a right mess when morning dawned. I managed to get back to my room before Alice got up and I had my shower and looked a damn sight better than Peter when he appeared downstairs.

He told Alice and George at breakfast that he hadn't really slept knowing that it was his last night before leaving home to go back to the university. George believed him but Alice didn't, knowing what went on between us. As George would be going to his bed, I offered to take Peter to the bus station, now having a valid driving licence and that's what I did.

On the way, I stopped and we had a kiss and cuddle as we said our goodbyes for we wouldn't be able to do it where other people would be around for the bus. He managed to dry his eyes before we got there and I stayed at the station until the bus left, giving him a wave which was returned from the window seat he had. The only consolation for me was that I would now be having sex with his mother every night, so I didn't feel as bad as he did. What I would be missing out is him fucking me, but at least I would still be getting my rocks off properly instead of masturbating.

Alice was like a tiger in bed that night, slobbering all over my erection and almost chewing the head as she attacked me. That was Saturday night and it was almost the same on Sunday with me giving her three orgasms to my two, once in her mouth and the other up in her pussy. So Monday was something of a respite what with the last night with Peter and the following two with Alice, I felt fucked and was glad to have a day off from sex. Though there was more looming in the background.

'I had Mike Winter speak to me the other day,' dad began at the dinner table that Monday evening, speaking to me. 'He's had such good reports about you and has seen some of the work you have done at other people's houses, that he'd like you to call around one evening and give him a quote on adding a small conservatory to the house.'

'Great! I'll do that,' pleased that the word was really getting around about my work.

'It made me quite proud of you with what he said.'

'Thanks, dad. I do my best every time,' I replied. He later gave me the address and I called around the following evening. The house was easy to find and I parked up and went and rang the bell and waited for it to be answered.

'Mr. Winter?' I asked of the man who opened the door.

'Yes,' was the reply.

'I'm Danny Rundene. You wanted to see me?' I asked of him.

'Yes, yes. Please come in,' and stepped aside to let me enter. He closed the door and took me into the lounge. 'This is my wife, Joyce.'

'Nice to meet you, Mrs. Winter,' I said, shaking her hand.

'Call me Joyce,' she said. 'It's less formal.'

'And my name's Mike,' he said shaking my hand, 'sit down please.' I went and sat down where indicated and he sat down next to me with a folder in his hand.

'Would you like a drink, Danny?' Joyce asked. 'Oh, you don't mind me calling you Danny, do you?'

'Er, not at all, er, Joyce. After all, it is my name,' I said and got a chuckle from Mike.

'Thank you but no, Joyce. I've just had my dinner and am rather full at the moment,' I told her and she then went and sat down in a chair opposite.

'Let me show you what we want,' he said, opening the folder and extracting a sketch of what they wanted. It was to be three sided, all glass, except the upright frames and a sloping glass tinted roof and sliding door. 'We'd also need a doorway made from the dining room through to the conservatory, sliding glass too.' There were some figures on all sides as the length, width and height that he wanted. I studied this for several minutes, picturing it in my mind.

'Er, the dimensions might have to change a little depending on the size of the glass and width of the uprights,' I began.

'No problem there,' he replied, and I carried on.

'I would suggest that the glass be double glazed if there's the likelihood of you using the place out of the summer season.'

'Fine.'

'It would take me about three to four weeks to construct but I would have to find out the cost of the materials, especially the glass before I could give you an exact cost. Those you will be shown and I'll only add on my labour costs plus the government tax of course. Give me a couple of days to get the right figures and then you can decide if we go ahead or not. Can I keep this sketch until then for it has the measurements on it?' I asked.

I saw him look over at his wife and saw her give a nod of her head and wondered to what she was nodding about, and found out a little later.

'Of course, and the time frame we'll leave to you. Come. Let me show you where we want it,' he said getting up as I did and followed him through to the dining room where he showed me where he wanted the access to be and then outside for me to get the placement in my mind.

'Now there's one other thing I would like to talk to you about in private,' he said as we re-entered the house. 'Let's go to my study,' and led me into another room and closed the doors. 'Would you like a drink now, for I need one with what I'm going to ask of you and I think you will want one too,' he said. An enigmatic remark and wondered why I would need a drink.

'Er, a beer would be fine if you have it,' I said.

'No problem. There's beer in my little fridge here,' he said, showing me where it was and he got out two cans and took two glasses off the shelf above it. He handed me both beer and glass and told me to sit down, which I did and had him sit opposite me. We opened the cans and filled up the glasses and he took a big gulp of his before holding the glass in both hands and leaned forward towards me.

'I…I'm not quite sure how you will react to what I am going to tell you, so please don't take offense as it is, er, rather difficult for me to actually say what I am going to say. What I am about to say is very personal and I must ask you not to repeat this to anyone. Absolutely no one. I'm not going to ask you to swear on the Bible for I think your word would be enough. Am I quite clear in what I have said so far.?'

'Er, yes sir, er Mike. I do understand,' I stammered, wondering what in hell is he going to say.

'My wife and I have talked this over for a year now and we have agreed to what I am going to say. I am now thirty one and my wife is twenty nine and we have been married for five years. Now the people who work at the plant, like your father, know that I was in an accident two years ago, though it's only the wife, our doctor and those at the hospital know exactly what happened to me. The accident itself is of no consequence but the result is.' His face was now somewhat on the red side and he took another big gulp of his beer, before continuing.

'Because of that accident, I lost my testicles. They had been crushed and so had to be removed.' Boy, that was taking the bull by the horns to tell me this, a virtual stranger. 'Now Joyce and I have always said that we would like to have a child or children, but is no longer the case for I am now unable to help in this.

We have heard a lot about you and we saw your picture in the local paper after saving that young girl from drowning and looked young and healthy and,' another gulp of beer, almost emptying the glass while I only took a sip waiting for the outcome, 'With us both now having met you, er, I don't really know how to say this properly, so I'll be rather blunt. Would you consent to taking on the task of making my wife pregnant, to give us a child that we could call our own and you not having any claim whatsoever as actually being the father? There! I've asked and can only hope for my wife's sake that your answer would be yes.' He sat back and found that his glass was almost empty and so got up and went and got another beer while I mulled over at how I've just had a bomb dropped in my lap.

He wanted me to fuck his wife, with her permission, to impregnate her, giving her a baby that I would never be able to call mine or say that I was the father. Fucking hell! My mind was reeling at what was being asked of me. Could I? Can I? Would I? The answer would be yes to the first two, but would I? That was the key question. I drained my glass without thinking and didn't even notice the glass being taken from my hand and only came back to the present when another full glass was pushed back into it. I nodded my thanks and drank half of it at one go.

'I…I'm somewhat flattered, Mike, but, can …can I listen to what, er, your wife, er, Joyce thinks of this proposal?' I managed to get out, hating myself for having stuttered.

'By all means, Danny. I just hope that I haven't upset you or caused any er, problems, church wise, in, er, what I must say is a rather outrageous request on our behalf. But believe me, it has been said from the heart. We both desire to have a child or children and are prepared to go to any lengths to have one. We both have admired your honesty said by those that we have talked to about you and believe that you have the heart and integrity to have listened to our plea and will honour us by being agreeable to our, er, what really is an outrageous request, but believe me, it has been asked in the hope that you would help us in having a child that we could call our own.'

With that said, he got up from his chair and I then followed him back to the sitting room where Joyce still sat in her chair as I went and knelt down beside her.

'Er, Joyce. I can call you Joyce?' I asked as an opener.

'Of course, Danny,' she replied.

'Your husband, Mike, has asked me to, er, help you have a baby. Is this your wish too?' I had by then taken hold of her hand and felt her give it a squeeze as her face went slightly red.

'Danny. We have been speaking of this for over a year now, and, and…it is with the agreement of us both that this is the only way now that we will ever have a child that we could call our own. To love and be loved as its mother and father. No one else needs to know that Mike is not the father, but it will be me that is the mother. God, for reasons of his own, took away what Mike had to do this for us and we've prayed that you might be the answer to grant us this ever dying wish that we could have a family. A child of our own that we could love and raise up to be as good as we believe you are.'

I nearly broke down into tears at this and felt very humbled in what she, no, they wanted out of life, and that was to have a child to love and cherish, albeit, acting as a surrogate father, and I could do no more than squeeze her hand and said that I would do what I could and hope that they would never regret what they had planned to do.

So in a nut shell. She wanted me to fuck her. Get her pregnant and then forget all about it. The birth and raising of whatever sex the child would be when she gave birth, would from that point on, have nothing to do with me.

There are many words that could and would describe me, but then the same could apply to them too, with me agreeing to this outrageous request, but one that I could see how their hearts were so intent of having a child or children. But then on reflection to what I have just said, that if they were happy with one child, they may want a sibling too for this one, whatever the sex was of this unborn or created child that they wished me to give them.

I have never been so humbled in my life at such request that I accepted to help them in this. You'll have to excuse me for I just cannot find the words to exactly say how I felt at this moment in time.

So it came to a verbal agreement, that even if they didn't accept my quote of the work they wanted doing on their conservatory, I was still wanted to impregnate Joyce with my seed to create a child for them. As it happened, they accepted my quote for the cost of the materials and my labour and I could start, on both jobs, when I was ready.

Of course, it wasn't something that I could tell Alice about, and I had decided that if and when I got to fuck Joyce, it would have to be in the afternoons. Now it would be at least a month between her menses to see if she had what is known as the woman's curse, and if this didn't happen. The odds were that I had indeed gotten her pregnant. So that was how it started with me bringing all, well most of the materials, to start work on the construction of their conservatory, and beginning the job; and at the end of the day's work, I then went inside the house to begin my other construction job. Read that as getting Joyce pregnant.

I must admit that it wasn't the best of beginnings, what with both of us being shy and not quite sure as to how exactly we should go about this coupling we were going to have. So I took the bull by the horns and took over. I had started on the foundations of this conservatory and in the late afternoon, told Mike that it was as far as I could go on that day and said that it was about time to start on what was wanted that to their mind was more important than what I had been doing out in the garden.

'It's embarrassing for me to say this, Danny, but Joyce is up in the bedroom waiting for you to…to..er.'

'Enough Mike. You don't have to say it. All I need is your blessing in what I am about to do, and in heavens name, do not take her to task in what we are about to do.'

'Danny, you have my blessing and with God's will, do and achieve what we both desire most in the world. God bless you.' I had no answer to this and then went upstairs to where Joyce was waiting for me.

I have never been so embarrassed in my life when I walked into their bedroom and seeing her there, lying on the bed with a nightdress on.

'Joyce. Please. If we are going to do this properly, please take off that night gown and be as naked as I will be in a few moments,' I said to her. Her face was already red and I'm sure it got even redder as she moved on the bed to take this gown off for me to see her lovely naked body there waiting for me.

Just the sight of this naked late twenty-year old married woman lying on the bed there, waiting for me to fuck her, was enough for my cock to rise up to its full potential. But it wasn't just going to be a wham-bam-thank-you-mam with me, I was going to give her the full work as shown to me by Alice.

Her eyes went wide when she saw my erection for the first time when I had divested myself of my clothing. I couldn't help the swinging of it from side to side as I approached the bed and got on to half lay on top of Joyce and asked if I could kiss her before we began. Her body, I felt, was tight beneath that part that covered her as she said yes, I could kiss her.

So with a soft kiss that was really only a caress on her lips, I began. She had, before I'd gotten on the bed, seen that I was up and hard, but now she could feel it pressing against her thigh as I kissed her. I then slowly kissed my way down her body, lingering for a while as I kissed each nipple and sucked and gave each a nibble before kissing the undersides and running my tongue around and beneath both of her lovely breasts. Just this was enough to have her body quivering and even more so when I tongued my way down to move through the soft and luxuriant pubic hair to tease the lips of her labia.

This tonguing was enough to make her legs open even wider for me to carry on using my tongue and fingers to enter and start teasing both clit and vagina. I heard her gasp at the first touch of my tongue moving over her clit and felt the tremor of her body and it began to relax as I started sucking on her and getting her to start releasing her fluids for me to suck into my mouth and excite her even more with my darting tongue in and out of her vagina.

I gave silent thanks to Alice in teaching me the art of cunnilingus and soon had Joyce squirming beneath me and knew that she was as close to an orgasm as she was going to get without me as of yet, entering her with my throbbing cock. I could have carried on and brought her to this orgasm of hers but the idea was to really get her pregnant, so I didn't carry on but lifted myself up until I was fully on top of her, letting her feel my cock at the entrance to her pussy.

Up onto my elbows, I went and pushed my hips forward and felt my fully erect cock enter and fill her. She gave out a gasp and her legs came up by my sides and her hands gripped my shoulders tight as I moved in until I could go no further. I stopped for a moment, loving the flexing of her muscles around my pulsating member before I really began fucking her.

She was already close before I had even entered her and now with me really fucking her, she began bucking herself beneath me and gave out one hell of a scream as she had her orgasm and it triggered me off into cumming inside her. Her bouncing me up and me driving her down with each thrust, drove her wild and had her clawing my back, hoping that she wasn't drawing blood which would be hard to explain to Alice later.

But I had now given her my sperm and hoped that at least some of it had evaded the downward rush of her juices, and had carried on to inseminate her and do what they were supposed to do in fertilizing an egg in her ovary.

'Oh Danny,' she gasped. 'I never dreamed it would be as good as this,' and pulled my head down to kiss me.

She didn't suck on my still hard and erect cock this first time when I pulled out of her, but later got her to give me a suck before and after cumming inside her, but that was later in the whole month that I fucked her. As it was, I pulled out of her and after giving her kiss, said thank you and got a kiss back, got up from the bed and went and had a shower to get rid of her smell that would have attached itself to my body, which I didn't want Alice to smell and know that I had been with another woman.

Leaving Joyce lying on the bed like a limp rag doll, I got dressed and after giving her a kiss, left the bedroom and went downstairs where Mike was waiting for me. He passed me an opened can of beer which I swallowed half in one go.

'Well?' he asked.

'Mike!' I cried. 'What do you want me to say? Whatever it is, I won't. I have done what you wanted me to do and that's it. It will still need more of this until we know that she is indeed pregnant. I can't really say anything at this first time, though I do have a question to ask you,' I said, and he could see that I was being slightly indignant.

'And what's that?' he asked.

'Has she ever sucked your cock?' was the first question, for I had another one to follow this.

'A couple of times,' he admitted, his face going slightly red at this blunt question. Wait for this one then, was my next thought.

'Have you ever been down and sucked on her?' was my second one.

'N...n...no,' he stuttered.

'Well you damn well should,' I said, getting a little angry with him. 'It's part of love making. If she will suck on you, you should at least reciprocate by doing the same back. I know that it will not do what you long for, but at least the pair of you should still be able to enjoy sex between you with you doing to her what she does to you,' I cried and then felt contrite. 'Sorry, Mike. I have spoken out of turn. It's not my place to tell you what you should and shouldn't do, I apologise. You can still have sex with her can't you?' I asked, and he nodded. 'Then give her what she wants in that line. Talk to each other and do what both of you want. Sorry, I'm speaking out of turn which is not my place to do so.'

'Danny,' he began, taking hold of my shoulders. 'You are quite right to chastise me and I will do as you say. I hope that this isn't going to stop you in what we have set out to achieve?'

'No, Mike. And it is I who should apologise for what I have said, for it's not my place to tell you people how to have a good sex life,' I told him quite contritely.

'You…you will still keep on trying then until… until, er, we know if she is or isn't?' he asked in a low voice.

'Of course, Mike. Just forget my outburst. It was unwarranted. Now go upstairs and tell her you love her, more so in what you are both trying to achieve,' I said.

I then left and went off to Peter's house where Alice was getting things ready for our dinner, George haven't as yet left his bed.

'How was your day with the new job?' she asked gaily.

'Tiresome and hadn't realised how difficult it is to build a conservatory,' I replied.

'But you will manage to do it right, won't you?' was the throw back question.

'Oh yes. I'm sure I've got my measurements right, that's the most important thing in any job you start,' I replied.

I was just going out of the kitchen to lay the table for dinner in the dining when George came in

'Evening, George,' I said as we passed.

'Evening,' he said, sounding a little grumpy. I carried on to the dining room but heard what he said to Alice.

'When's he moving back to his own house?' George asked Alice.

'Now don't be like that George. I enjoy his company of an evening so I'm not alone. Besides, he buys all my groceries at the weekend, so he's paying his way. Also, I feel safer at night with a man in the house and not being all alone. He's got his own room to sleep in....'

'And I hope he stays in it,' George said, still sounding grumpy.

'That he does,' Alice sprang back at him, sounding angry now, 'every night! So don't start getting funny ideas for you'd be wrong. As I said, he's company for me of an evening and knows his place, so let's not hear anymore of him moving out. Besides, Peter likes him being here and looking after the workshop.'

I felt a little embarrassed at dinner, but George didn't say a word of what he had said to Alice and he didn't bring it up again, well not in my hearing.

In bed that night with naked Alice in my arms, I told her that I had overheard what they had said, about my company and sleeping in my own room.

'Well it's true,' she giggled, stroking my cock that had not long been up in her pussy. 'You're always in your own bed at night.'

'And you not saying that you were in it too,' I said, rolling her over and fucking her again and giving her another orgasm.

'I love you, Danny,' she whispered in my ear after we'd finished. 'You can stay here as long as you like, I'll see to that,' so after a few more kisses, we finally fell asleep.

I carried on with my work at the Winter's place and giving the foundations a day or two to really be dry and solid, knocked a hole in the wall of the dining room and put in the sliding window doors which took up the whole day. This had to be done first so that I could then see at what height the conservatory floor had to be so that there wouldn't be any kind of steps between the two rooms.

'You've done a fine job with these doors,' Mike said as he slid one back and forth. 'I think you need a shower now and Joyce is in the bedroom waiting for you.'

'What did Joyce say about yesterday?' I asked.

'Well she had been a bit apprehensive at first, but said that when, er, when you got started, everything went okay,' he said.

'I'm glad of that then,' I told him.

'I…I think that she actually enjoyed it,' he stammered.

'Did, er, did you and Joyce, er, you know, make love afterwards?' I finally got out.

'Oh yes. I can still get an erection and have er, what's known as a dry orgasm. Not cumming. So my body still reacts as though I've still got my nuts. Er, as…as to what you told me yesterday, I wasn't sure exactly what you meant and with her saying that it was good. Er, can, er, will you let me watch and see precisely what you did to please her. You know, er like a teacher but not say anything but just do it and let me see it being done. Actions are better that words,' he trailed off with, his face rather on the red side at asking if he could watch.

I had read in one of Peter's dirty books that some men get turned on by seeing their wife being fucked by another man, so I agreed if Joyce agreed too. To this she had agreed, he told me, and so we both went upstairs and into their bedroom where Joyce was already in bed, waiting for me. I saw Mike move the dressing table stool to a corner of the room as I went into the bathroom to have a shower before joining Joyce in bed.

In the shower washing myself, I got a perverse thrill run through me at the thought of having him there to see me fuck his wife and it brought on an erection that I still had after drying myself and walking back into the bedroom. I couldn't see his face in the gloom of the corner and had to put him out of my mind as I pulled back the bed sheet to reveal Joyce's naked body waiting for me.

So I began my love making to Joyce by kissing her before moving down to kiss and playing with the nipples of her breasts and then carrying on down to get between her legs and suck and tease her pussy, starting the build up to her having an orgasm. When I felt she was ready, I moved back up on top of her and after raising myself up on my elbows, entered and fucked her.

It was lovely having her legs tight to my waist with them up in the air, her hands holding onto my shoulders as I pounded into her, bringing her up to crying out at her orgasm and triggering me off to give her my cum in the hope that at least one of the little buggers made it to the ovaries to fertilise an egg.

She didn't suck on me after I pulled out this time what with Mike watching, though she did later with him being in the room with us. After giving her a kiss, I got off the bed and got dressed and left the room with Mike following me downstairs.

'Wow!' he exclaimed. 'I didn't think that I would get a hard on at seeing my wife being fucked, but I did, and still got it. I also got the impression that when you pulled out that she would have sucked on you, but didn't. Maybe it was because I was there. Did she do it the first time?

'No. But like you, I think she wanted to,' I replied. 'Would you mind if she did?'

'No, I don't think so,' he said.

'Do you think that she might want you to take an active part with you being in the room and seeing me make love to her. I mean,' and my heart was in my mouth. 'I mean like if you got a hard on at seeing us together, she'd feel a bit better if she saw me sucking on you?' There, I had said it, trying to draw him into it being more of a threesome than him just being a voyeur, a looker on.

'You mean you'd suck my cock?' he asked, his eyes opening wider.

'Well you've still got a hard on at watching us and you did say that you still go through the process of having a dry orgasm, would you like me to?' I asked.

'Er, well, if you want to. It'll be a new experience for me never having had a man suck on me before,' he said, his face red again.

'Sit down and enjoy it,' I said. So he sat down, a bemused expression on his face as I got down onto my knees between his legs, resting my elbows on his thighs and pulled down the zipper of his trousers and put my hand inside and felt his hard cock and pulled it out into the open. 'It's a nice looking cock you've got, Mike,' I said just before I took the head of it into my mouth. He gave out a gasp at me doing this and was able to push the foreskin down with my lips and then tongued his G-spot making his body shudder.

His cock was about the same size as Peter's and I liked sucking on his. Well I liked sucking a cock anyway so I now enjoyed having another one in my mouth to suck and gently chew on. The only difference would be not getting a different taste of cum for Mike was unable to give any, but I still had the thrill of sucking on him. Especially when he started bucking his hips up towards me and went through the throes of having his non existing orgasm, coming to a shuddering stop and felt his body relax under my arms on his upper thighs.

'That was incredible,' he gasped. 'It really felt as though I did cum in your mouth. Thank you, Danny, thank you.' I gave the head of his still hard cock a kiss before pushing it back inside his trousers.

'Would you like me to do that in front of Joyce tomorrow? Then maybe she would then suck on mine, though I think you'd better talk this over first for she might not want to see you being sucked on.' I left it there rather than say too much for it was now up to him.

I got up from my knees as he got up out of the chair, both of us with smiles on our faces and he saw me to the door where we said our goodbyes but didn't kiss for he might not have wanted that. I got into the pick-up and drove off to Peter's house quite happy in having fucked Joyce and now having sucked on Mike and later would be sucking and fucking Alice in my bed.

So I was a happy man having a cock to suck now, wondering if he would ever ask if he could fuck me with it. A woman who wanted me to get her pregnant and another woman, Alice, who I would not be able to get in the same state, though not from the lack of trying.

I kept my end up that night with Alice, pun intended, and gave her three orgasms to my two, one in her mouth and the other while in her pussy, a very good night for both of us. But I was looking forward to finding out what Mike and Joyce had said between them after I had left, and so did quite a bit of laying the floor of the conservatory the next day, well not the floor really but the under build of it before the final top layer, telling Mike that no one should walk on it until I said so.

It had been a good days work and Mike offered me a beer in the kitchen which I accepted and almost downed it in one go I was that thirsty.

'Did you and Joyce talk things over last night?' I asked.

'Yes, and she was surprised that you said that you would suck on me if she sucked on you,' he said.

'Did you tell her that I had sucked on you last night?' I asked.

'No, but I did say that I had been aroused at seeing the pair of you make love with me watching,' he said. I could only shrug my shoulders for it was down to him and not me to really start the ball rolling on a threesome. He gave out a little laugh as we moved off to go upstairs. 'I've even started to get a hard on already and you haven't even started yet.' I grinned back at him and followed him into the bedroom. It was the same as the previous afternoon by going for a shower first and returning to the bedroom with my erection leading the way. I got a lovely smile from Joyce and I got onto the bed and did the same again of sucking her pussy first before fucking her.

I took a quick glance over to where Mike was sitting and saw that he had his erect cock out of his trousers and was slowly moving his hand up and down the shaft as he watched me fucking his wife. Well I believed I would then be sucking it in front of her afterwards, but pushed that back in my mind as I strove to hold back my cumming until Joyce had her second orgasm. Thankfully it wasn't long in coming and with her really bucking up beneath me, I was then able to let go and give her my cum.

With her body relaxing, I came to a stop, my cock still throbbing inside her as our sweaty chests met, both of us panting quite heavily. I could see the sweat on her forehead, but it was her sparkling eyes that caught mine, and also smiling up at me.

'I hope that what we are doing is going to work,' she panted.

'For your and Mike's sake, I hope so too, though I have loved being with you,' I said, me breathing much like she was. 'Have you spoken with Mike about how many times we will be coupling?' I thought it better worded that way instead of saying about us having a fuck.

'Another couple of times and then we wait to find out if it has worked,' she said which was disappointing news for me as I was enjoying this afternoon sex with Joyce in spite of her husband watching us.

But now I rose up and pulled out of her and saw that Mike had taken his trousers off and he now came and lay down beside Joyce and I rolled onto my side to take hold of his erection and took the head of his cock into my mouth and began to suck on him for the second time. I came to a sudden stop when I felt the hand of Joyce take hold of my cock and take the head of mine into her mouth and start sucking out any residue of my cum, not missing out on her own juices either.

So after five afternoons of fucking Joyce, a halt was called on this though I still had two weeks work to do in building their conservatory. I'm proud to say that they were over the moon when inspecting the finished work and they couldn't thank me enough. Mike took quite a few pictures of the finished work, adding these to others that he had taken during the whole process. He was kind enough to give me copies, some of which I could then use in a portfolio I was building of my work. This could then be shown to other people who wanted to know my work before giving me a job.

It was during this last week that I was told that Joyce had missed the expected day of the start of her usual menstruation and they would give it another two weeks before seeing their doctor to find out if she was pregnant or not. The news was that she was indeed pregnant and I was thanked again by the pair of them.

Forgive me for I will now jump ahead to finish this off about Joyce and Mike Winter, by saying that during the time of her pregnancy, she had several scans to see that everything was as it should be, but did not want to know the sex of the baby that she was carrying until the birth.

The time duly arrived of her going into labour and the result was them now having a daughter. With them then knowing the sex of the baby, said that as it was me that helped them in this, that they wanted me to give it a name, an honour which I didn't really deserve for I had fun creating her, but agreed to their request and gave them the name Alice. I think you can work out why that was the name I gave them.

But it didn't all end there! A year later, they asked if I would help them again as they wanted a son. I was flattered to be asked but said that there was no way that I could guarantee that but they had found out that if Joyce had some male hormones injected into her womb, the likelihood was very possible. Anyway, I agreed, for she had been a good fuck and I looked forward to another five sessions with her and also getting to suck on Mike's dry dick.

This came to pass as our mutual enjoyment and she did in fact then give birth to a boy and again I was asked to give him a name and chose Peter, which they liked and agreed to, so I was again, absentia parentis, somewhat mangling my Latin.

But back to the present. The life that I was leading was wonderful. I had work which brought in money, had my meals cooked and my washing done, and a lovely woman to fuck at night in bed. Almost like being married. The bonus being that after every twelve weeks, I had Peter to fuck and have him fuck me, albeit, only for a short period and it made me think about the future when he graduated from the university. This, I didn't want to even think about at this time, so I put it to the back of my mind and would deal with this when the time came.

My twentieth birthday arrived, and with it being on a Monday this particular year, meant that I wouldn't have Peter attend it though his dad George could. For it was a grand barbecue out in the back garden of my own house and had not only Alice and George there, but some other friends of the family attended.

As the guests arrived, I don't know if George noticed it or not, but all the females that came, gave me a birthday kiss on the cheek whereas with Alice, it was on the lips. If he had, nothing was said and I don't think my parents noticed it either. It was a grand party and it wasn't until midnight, that people started to say their goodbyes for a wonderful party. I was getting kissed again but with a slight difference. What with the drinks that had been consumed, quite a few women, married or not, kissed me on the lips and saw in some, certain looks in their eyes that they would have liked to have gone further.

Poor Peter. His birthday was due two weeks after mine and he would still be at the university and on his own, except for maybe a few friends, but it wouldn't be the same not being at home. So I made a decision and phoned him to say that I would come up to where he was for that special day. He was delighted at this, saying that he was now really looking forward to it. I made sure that I was free from work on that day and the following one and when it arrived, told Alice and George what I was going to do. About being there for his birthday and not about having sex with him, though Alice guessed that I would.

I was up early and drove to the airport and left the pick-up in the parking lot and went and got a ticket for my destination and a return for the following day. It was a two-and-half-hour flight and so it was late morning when I arrived, but not having any luggage, was soon off and getting one of the first taxis in the line to take me to the university.

There was one motel that I noticed on our journey into town that had a diner close by and a decent, well from the outside, a decent-looking restaurant, and decided that we would spend the night at this motel. On arriving at the university, I had the driver wait while I collected another passenger and went in to the main office and asked for a call to be made for Peter Denton to come to this office. The secretary did this and with him knowing that I was coming, was with me within five minutes.

'Happy Birthday, Peter,' I cried upon seeing him and we went and hugged each other, no kisses for the woman behind the counter could see us, a hug was nothing between friends, but a kiss would have been going a bit too far.

'Thanks for coming, Danny. You really have made my day,' he said as I led him out and down to the waiting taxi. I then, on entering the cab, told the driver to drop us off at the diner next to the motel that I had spotted and within 20 minutes we were there. I paid him off and we went into the diner to order takeaway burgers and fries, having told Peter that we would book into the motel a few yards down the highway.

Carrying our bags of food, walked down there where I went and showed my driving licence and booked us both into the same room saying that we were brothers, signing the registration book as Danny and Peter Rundene. Collecting the key to the room offered, we went and it wasn't until we were inside, did we go into a clinch to hug and kiss each other.

We decided to prolong the agony we both felt in wanting to couple together in sex, to eat our burgers and fries, and tell each other what we both had been doing over the past few weeks. His was boring and mine, well you know of that but for Peter, I left out about Alice, Joyce and Mike. Our lunch, if you could call it that, was soon eaten and we then began to kiss and get each other's clothes off for us to go straight into the sixty nine position and suck on the erect cock that faced us. The sucking of Peter instead of Mike was different which is obvious with the contents of Peter's balls flooding my mouth as he cummed, taking mine too, for us to enjoy moving the mass of semen around our mouths before swallowing and then licking and sucking again until both cock heads where clean.

It was mostly incoherent drivel that we spoke in between kisses as we stroked and fondled each other on one of the beds in the motel until we had both risen up again to be full erection and ready for use.

'You're ready now, lover. Fuck me. Fuck my pussy and make me happy,' he had said. Now where or when in hell did he start calling his ass his pussy? Was he becoming more of a female than male? Or did he……? Forget that! You don't want to know, my mind shouted out to me. Whether he did or didn't, doesn't concern you, it cried out again. You've been fucking other people, his mother included, it said, so drop the thoughts. This I did and saw that he was now lying on his back and not on his knees as we were used to having sex in this position.

'Why this way?' I asked, looking down at him as I knelt there between his legs.

'So that I can see the expressions on your face as we fuck. To see that smile as you cum inside me and so that we can kiss with you still throbbing inside me. I want it bare back so I can feel it when you do cum inside me, and I can also hold you and know that you love me as we kiss.' All doubts had gone now.

'You've had sex with another male,' I said, still not having moved. His face went red and he nodded.

'Only twice, Danny,' he said, his voice more of a whine. 'I wanted you but, well, there was another who wanted it and you were not there. Oh darling, I'm sorry,' and he started to cry. 'Oh Danny, I wanted you so badly but I wasn't strong enough to resist. I made believe that it was you, truly,' he sobbed.

'You used a condom I hope?' I asked.

'Of course, Danny. I insisted on that for I knew that the only one that I really wanted was you, fucking me bare back, but I wouldn't let him. A condom or not at all, and when he produced one and saw the cock that he had, I couldn't say no,' his body now shaking and tears flowing down his face. 'His...his,' and he hiccupped. 'He wasn't as big as you, but just seeing it there.....' and off he went again, sobbing. Boy, he really knew how to tug at my heart strings. I fell forward onto him and kissed him, trying to wipe the tears away at the same time as we kissed, both feeling the erections we had now being squashed between us.

'There, Peter, there,' I said as I stroked his face. 'As long as a condom was used, I forgive you.' Hypocrite! My mind screamed at me. You've not been going without sex over the same period of time! 'So you had sex in this fashion, lying on your back?'

'Yes,' he whispered. 'But it was your face that I saw each time and wished, oh how I wished that it had been you. I'm sorry, Danny,' and he started to cry again.

'So you are as a woman having sex lying on your back then?' I asked softly.

'Yes, Danny. I am the woman for you. I want you. I need you! Fuck me and let me know that it is you by seeing your face. Your smiling face as you fuck your wife!' he said.

Christ! He was my wife now? Not just a lover, but my wife! Well it was him that had really started us off into being lovers, what with his male pictures up on the wall of the workshop and wanting me to be the first to fuck him. I can't answer as to why I let him fuck me in return. Quid pro Quo?

'Well, Peter, as you used a condom, we can make love without one,' I said as I lifted my body up off of his and he gave me a smile that said so many words that it would takes pages to say what I read in his eyes that had lit up knowing by my words that I had forgiven him and not refused to fuck him or moved away from him.

He arched his back so that he could lift his legs right up for his lower calves to rest on my shoulders. This action and movement also lifted his ass up from the bed and I could just see it there, high enough for me to put my cock inside to fuck him. I leaned forward to support myself on my outstretched arms either side of his body, bending it forward a little more and knew by the touch, as he gave out a shiver, that the head of my cock was in the right place.

I leaned in closer, feeling my cock start to expand his ring piece and with a gasp from him, entered into the hot and tight interior of his ass. Forever forward it seemed that I moved into him, his legs starting to slide down my arms to rest in the crook of the elbows as I filled him till I couldn't go any further.

'I love you, Danny,' he smiled up at me as my cock throbbed away inside him, his muscle flexing itself round the shaft of my cock. 'I love where you are and that it is you that's now inside me. Take me to heaven.'

I couldn't help but smile back down at him as I began to fuck him in this new position for us. Him smiling back at me, pursing his lips in a kiss as I fucked my "wife." Half way through, I stopped and really leaned forward to him and had his hands come round my neck to help lift him up so that we could have a kiss before I carried on until I reached my peak and really began to ram myself into him, hearing his cries and the pleasure on his face as he felt every shot of my cum into his pussy as he called it.

The only trouble was that with him half bent at the middle as he was, his own throbbing cock up high on his stomach, began to jerk and pulsate and as I came inside him, he let fly with his cum, shooting out of the eye of his cock and coating his chest in a stream of this milky fluid. It reached up to his chin that first shot, the rest just adding to the line of cum that he had laid down.

Bang goes his fucking of me, was the thought in my mind as I saw it shooting out as I cummed inside him. I wanted that, my mind cried out, up my ass like he's getting mine. But it was too late now crying over spilt milk and had to choke back the laugh that this thought had come into my mind.

'Oh Danny,' he wailed. 'Look what I've done, and I didn't even touch myself.'

'Don't worry about it,' I said as I eased myself down to lay on top of him with me still being buried inside him. His legs had slid down now though still wide apart and I kissed him, feeling his sperm being smeared over our chests. 'You must have needed me so much. You should have fucked me first and we wouldn't have this mess between us.

Well we can still lick it off,' and with his body relaxing and starting to straighten out, I felt myself slipping out of him.

With some effort on his part, he heaved me up and rolled me off of him where he then began licking his cum up off my chest. I then did the same to him before I got up from the bed to go and wash my cock from where it had been before returning and having him kiss me and snuggle up into my arms.

'I love you, Danny,' he whispered in my ear. 'Love you with all my heart.'

'I love you too, Peter and I forgot to buy a birthday present before coming up here,' I said to him.

'You've just given me the best present that I could wish for,' his hand moving down and stroking my soft cock.

'That's not enough,' I answered him.

'It's big and more than enough for me,' he replied.

We kissed and stroked each other, saying silly love things to each other for the next hour until his handling of me brought me up to another erection. Mind you, I brought his up too and so we slipped into the sixty-nine position to suck on each other, briefly stopping to tell him that I wanted him to cum in my ass and not in my mouth. So we soon stopped this and then had the pleasure of once again having him behind and fucking me. Then I got his cum in the place where I wanted it, feeling it coat my insides with every pulsating salvo that made me quiver with delight.

I then fucked him in the doggie position which I preferred before we went and had a shower before I took him to the restaurant that I had seen just past the diner. We had an excellent dinner to celebrate his birthday, drinking a bottle and a half each of wine between us before going back to the motel for more sexy loving.

When we were naked, I had him kneel on the edge of the bed so that I could stand up behind him, slowly pushing my cock up into his ass and slowly moving my erection in and out at a leisurely pace, which didn't exhaust me as much as acting the dog with its bitch. He crooned with delight as he felt my cum hitting him and I just loved pumping my seed up into his tight backside.

When it was my turn to be the recipient of his cock and cum, I was on my knees as usual and gurgled in pleasure when I felt him fill me with his cock until his thighs were up against the cheeks of my bum.

'Ease yourself down onto your front, Danny,' he said, 'and let my lie on your back as we fuck. It really tightens up your insides around my cock and it's lovely.' This I did. Slowly falling forward with him holding on to me and staying inside until I was flat out while he was on top of me and still had his throbbing cock inside me. He was right, for I could feel that I had tightened up inside and with him getting his hands up under my shoulders to grip tightly, using this as a means of heaving himself up to fuck me. His cock never seemed to leave my body as he fucked me in this fashion with just his hips moving as he pulled himself into me. It was tight and lovely and had him cum in quite a short time in this position.

After our shower, we were back on the bed and sucked on each other's balls and nibbled at the cock in front of us as well as giving it some sucking until these were both up and hard. We carried on until we both gave up our cum to be savoured before swallowing, but still kept on sucking away and I think we both fell asleep in doing this, with us both sucking on a cock like a child with a pacifier in our mouths.

We woke up in this position though I can't say who woke up first, but we carried on where we had left off and soon, with the morning erection, had us cumming into each other which was as good as that first cup of coffee in the morning. We couldn't stay there any longer as he still had his classes to attend and so we showered and didn't have time for breakfast and had the motel clerk phone for a cab to take us first to the university and then to the airport. We had kissed our goodbyes before leaving the motel room for we wouldn't be able to do that outside, so with the cab arriving, I gave up the room key, having paid last night, we were driven off to the University. Sitting in the back, we were able to stroke each other's thigh and crotch and I think we both got hard inside our trousers. Well I did and so didn't get out of the cab when we dropped Peter off. It was just a squeeze of the hand and he waved goodbye as the cab pulled away to drive me to the airport.

After paying him off, I had to go straight to the men's toilets to get into a cubicle and jerk myself off as I had stayed hard for the whole journey. So having reduced my cock to its flaccid state, checked in and was soon being flown back to my home airport. I had kept this day free of work and so I got into my pick-up and drove off to Peter's house and within half an hour, I was on the sofa with Alice in the workshop.

With us both naked, stroking and caressing each other, we kissed first before speaking.

'How's Peter? Did he enjoy his birthday?' she asked.

'He was over the moon with me turning up, and yes, we both enjoyed his birthday,' I told her with a smile.

'I guessed you would,' she replied smiling back at me.

'Though I'm glad to be back here with you,' I said kissing her and then started to really make love to her by moving my body down over hers until I was between her thighs and giving her the first orgasm of the day. I didn't get a chance to finish the job of cleaning her up because she was tugging at my ears.

'Now, Danny, now! Fuck me!' I finally heard her crying out. Her thighs had opened, letting me get free and I quickly slid my body up hers, our sweat creating a lovely smooth slope, reaching out with my hands either side of her chest to heave myself up and feel my throbbing cock slide up into her pussy like a knife through butter. Into the inner body heat and feeling her muscle moving faster than a sewing machine as it flexed itself along my probing cock. She gave out a gasp as our pubes met and the smile she gave me was something to die for as I came to a stop. Her chest was heaving beneath me and saw that through the sweat, her nipples were up and as hard as gold nuggets.

My problem now was that I was ready to let myself go at any time, but wanted her to cum at the same time. So I was using the deep thrust then a short thrust, a technique from the east though I can't remember what it's called. With the short thrust, you actually pull your cock right out of the pussy you're fucking, letting it spring up on exit to rasp her clit before then giving her the deep thrust. Well it worked with my cock hitting her clit every second inward push for she was soon beginning to buck herself beneath me.

So in less than a minute, her legs were squeezing my waist as she almost lifted us both off the sofa as she had her orgasm, then letting go of mine to then fill her before coming to a stop with sweat pouring down from my forehead and chest.

'That's…that's…the best…yet, Danny,' she panted, her chest heaving, making her hard nipples press themselves to my chest with every deep breath she took. I smiled down at her, seeing that she was as sweaty as I felt and knew that the next stop would be the showers for us both. Different rooms of course in case George woke up. Well she must have woken him up for I heard his voice after I had showered, but now knowing that he was awake, went back into my room and changed into working gear and went down and out into the garden and carried on with mowing the lawns.

I worked until Alice called out that dinner was ready, so stopped, washed my hands and joined them at the table and after the meal, carried on to finish the mowing of the lawns. It was just getting dark then and so by the time I'd had my shower, it was time for bed. I'd already told Alice what I was doing and so she knew when to come to my room where we had a nice leisurely coupling that we both enjoyed enormously. Our second session was almost a replica of the first and it really tired us both and it wasn't long after breaking apart that we fell asleep.

It was two days later that I had a strange encounter. I was called to a job that was at the other side of town to where I was based, but having some free time, I went. It was a stupid little job that only took an hour and a half but they paid me, including my fuel costs for the work done and not having even been offered a drink there, I was thirsty and so stopped at the first diner I came to. With the time being between breakfast and lunch, the place was almost empty. Only two tables of four being inside and I went and sat down at a two-seater by the window.

There were two waitresses there and as I sat down, one came towards me with a tray of two milk shakes and two coffees on it for a table past mine. As she came almost level with mine, a youngster at a table almost opposite me suddenly stood up without looking. Sod's law stepped in and his head hit a corner of the tray that this waitress was carrying, knocking it out of her hand.

Guess where it landed? Correct! Right in my fucking lap. Two milk shakes and two white coffees hit the lower part of my T shirt and flooded the front of my shorts. Pandemonium as I gave out a shout at the shock of it all landing in my lap. The waitress gave out a scream. The boy shouting out that it wasn't his fault and the adults with him quickly got him out of the diner as the waitress who had lost the tray was trying to pick up what she could from my lap.

All she kept saying was sorry as she tried, but with me standing up, sent most of it to the floor.

'Fuck!' was all I could say, trying to stop her hand that held a cloth from trying to wipe down my front.

'Sorry, sir, sorry,' and then pulled my arm. 'Come out back and let me get you cleaned up. Rosie?' she called out to the other girl. 'See to that tables order while I see to this gentleman,' still pulling at my arm. I gave up and followed her, shaking the front of my shorts as we went through a side door and she led me to what appeared to be the staff toilet. She pulled me inside and shut the door.

'I'm terribly sorry about that, sir. My name is Maisie. Now get those wet things off and let me clean them.' I couldn't think of anything but getting my wet T-shirt off. This I did and she took it and put it on the edge of the basin in there. 'Shorts as well,' she said and saw me hesitate. 'Oh come on! I've seen a naked man before. Get those shorts off.'

Such was my confusion at what had happened and at the speed that I was hustled out and into this toilet and the authoritive way that she spoke, I did as I was told and took them off, sitting down onto the toilet seat to get the shorts down over my boots. She had knelt down to help me get them off over my boots and looked at what had been uncovered.

'Well that's a nice cock you've got there, covered in coffee. Stand up!' she commanded as she got up and put my shorts along with my T-shirt, seeing them slip to the floor which she seemed to ignore. She then, with the same cloth she had tried to clean me up at first, having brought it in with her, soaked it under the tap and began to use it to wipe my front.

All this had happened within a couple of minutes and with her moving about so fast, I had no chance of stopping her from what she was doing. Now with my cock and balls being washed with a wet cloth or without, my body reacted as it always did when being handled, and started to rise up to an erection.

'Wow! I haven't seen one this big,' she said when it was fully erect. 'Sit down,' pushing me back and being caught off balance fell back to finish sitting on the toilet with my prick standing out proud from my groin. 'I can't let this go,' she said standing in front of me and pulled up her short black skirt so that it was around her waist, and I saw the white panties she was wearing beneath it. She was quick, no two ways about it, for she straddled my thighs and with one hand, pulled the gusset of her panties to one side and used the other hand to take hold of my rigid cock and hold it upright as she then sank down on it.

Her internal body heat was like an inferno as she took me inside her pussy, sinking down until she was sitting on my thighs.

'Christ! It feels bigger that it looked,' she said, wiggling her hips on my thighs, making the head of my cock rub both sides of her vagina that was buried deep inside her. Then she started bouncing up and down on me as her hands held onto my shoulders. My hands had automatically gone to her waist to help her in this technical fucking on my rampant cock.

It had all happened so quick with her mounting me that there was nothing that I could now do but help her in what she was doing, besides, I was now enjoying it. She then gave out a cry and really pulled our bodies together and held me tight as her body began to shudder, me knowing that she was having an orgasm and of course, with my cock where it was and what was being done to it, cummed into her at the same time, me shuddering the same way she had.

'Wow!' she panted, leaning her head onto my shoulder. 'I haven't cum like that for ages,' she panted, her breath hot against my neck. 'Nor have I had a cock like yours inside me. Wrong that it is, I'm kind of glad of the accident we had outside there,' and she kissed me. 'Bloody hell!' she then cried out. 'We've just had a fuck and I don't even know your name.'

'Danny,' I said, now holding her in a hug, making my cock twitch inside to her little giggles as she felt it.

'You certainly are some cocksman,' she came back at me and surprised me again by suddenly lifting herself off of me and quickly went down onto her knees and sucked on my wet cock. Only for a minute or two before getting up and pulling down her skirt. 'Let me now see to cleaning your shorts and T-shirt,' she said, picking them up from the floor.

'Forget the -shirt,' I said as she was leaving the toilet. 'I've never liked it.' She gave me a smile and shut the door. I still sat there, both stunned and shocked that in that short time from having the coffee and milk shakes in my lap, I'd had a woman fuck herself on my cock before leaving me on my own. I had to give my head a shake to bring me back to reality and knew that I would have to wash myself for it wouldn't do with Alice smelling as well as tasting another woman's juices on and around my cock when we bedded later that evening. So I got up and gave my groin, cock and balls a damn good wash in the basin and dried myself on the paper towels that were there.

I was now clean but still bollock naked, except for my boots and went to the door and opened it to see Maisie giving my shorts a shake.

'Are they dry yet?' I asked.

'No. I just got the front clean and have yet to dry them,' she said.

'Well have you got a towel or something that I can cover myself with?' I asked her.

'No,' and she looked around and picked up my T shirt. 'Use this to cover yourself and come out here and sit down,' she said as she threw me my dirty T-shirt. I caught it and looked outside the door to see if anyone else was there, and saw another man, obviously the cook working at a grill with his back towards me, and so I quickly scuttled across to where Maisie was and sat down on a chair that was near her, covering my front with the shirt I held in my hand. 'I can't get all the stains out but at least it's not sticky. Here, hold it while I get out the electric fire to dry it. What did you come in the diner for? Whatever it was, it's on the house.'

'Er, just a bacon sandwich and a coke,' I said. She then turned around.

'Joe!' she shouted at the man at the grill. 'One bacon sandwich for this hunk sitting here, oh, and a coke.' She then disappeared through another door and came back a minute later with and electric fire and a coat hanger. She plugged the fire in near that door and took my shorts from my hand and fixed it to the hanger which was then hung on the door knob and turned on the fire and got it closer to my shorts for the heat to dry it. She then collected my sandwich and coke and gave it to me. 'On the house. Back in a mo',' and off she went after giving me a big smile.

I sat there drinking my coke and eating my sandwich still bemused at how fast she had organised things and of us having that fuck in the toilet as I watched the slight steam coming up from my drying shorts. She came back about ten minutes later and took my empty plate and can from me and put them by the sink and came and felt my shorts.

'It's dry now,' she said and took it off the hanger and passed it to me. 'Don't be shy now,' giving me that smile again. 'I've seen it, felt it, sucked it and, well, if ever you feel that you need a good fuck again, call in anytime and I'll help you out.' She pulled the T-shirt away from me so that she could see again what I had between my legs as I got up and put my shorts back on. With her previous comment, my cock had started to rise up again, but quickly covered it with my warm shorts.

'Er, thanks, Maisie, for…for my sandwich and drink, and….er what you have done for me.'

'You're welcome,' she said and gave me a kiss. 'Do come back sometime for us to have it again.'

'I'll keep you in mind, Maisie, and thanks again,' I said and then went and left the diner wondering if I would go back sometime, but doubtful that I would since it is at the opposite side of town.

I drove my pick-up back towards Peter's house, thinking of how erotic it had been, sitting on the toilet seat naked with my cock standing upright, her pulling up her skirt and pulling aside the gusset of her panties before impaling herself on my rampant cock.

I parked up by the garage, leaving enough room for George to get his car out when he went off to work later and was surprised to see him already up when I entered the kitchen. No sex with Alice in the workshop then.

'You're back early,' George said from where he was sitting at the kitchen table.

'Yeah. Stupid woman. I thought I had a major disaster to repair, but it didn't take long,' I replied, accepting the cup of coffee that Alice had poured out for me, giving her my thanks, looking at the wan smile on her face and knew why it was so. George and I sat there talking for a good two hours, the longest I'd ever talked with him I think. Not knowing that I would not have the chance again for we had the most calamitous thing that could ever happen to a household a few nights later.

Alice and I had had a lovely evening in my bed, licking, sucking and fucking before going to sleep but were woken up just after three in the morning with the doorbell being pushed quite a few times. Long rings at that.

'What the fuck's that?' Alice said on waking up at the continuing ring of the bell.

'Don't know,' I replied, awake too and saw what the time was. 'Whoever's there is insistent. Let me answer the door,' I said, getting out of bed as she did too, putting on her gown and I got mine out of the bathroom, put it on, went downstairs with Alice following me.

'Okay! I'm coming,' I shouted out as I was going down and the bell stopped ringing at hearing my voice. I got to the door and opened it to find two police officers standing there.

'Mr. Denton?' the one in front asked of me.

'No. I'm a guest here,' I replied.

'Is Mrs. Denton here then?' he asked.

'I'm Mrs. Denton,' Alice said from behind me.

'May we come in?' he asked and I knew then that there had been trouble, and with it being this early in the morning, guessed that involved George.

'Ye…yes,' Alice stammered, and I stood aside to let the two of them enter and saw that Alice's face had gone a deathly white.

'Please sit down, Mrs. Denton,' this first officer said, pointing to the sofa. Alice seemed to stagger as she went and sat down and I moved and sat down beside her and took hold of her hand as both policemen came and stood in front of us.

'It's bad news I'm afraid. Your husband has been killed in a gunfight at the plant.' A bald and shocking statement really, but there was no point of beating about the bush with this kind of news.

'Oh my God. No!' Alice cried out, her other hand raised up to her mouth, tears coming from her eyes and her other hand squeezing mine tight. I managed to get my other arm around her shoulders as she began to quiver and shake.

'I'm afraid so. His partner was also shot and is in a very serious condition now at the hospital. Along with one of the other gunmen. Three of them had been killed too. It looks like they were raiding the plant and were stopped by your husband and his partner and put up a good fight and stopped them.'

At least the police officer had a sorrowful look on his face as did the other one.

'Sorry to be the bearer of this tragic news, but you had to be told,' he said.

'Where…where is my husband now?' Alice stammered, choking back the sobs and tears.

'At the city morgue now, and I'm afraid that later you will have to confirm his identity,' he said.

'I can't believe it,' Alice said in a low voice, and I hugged her tight to me to stop her shivering. 'I just can't believe it.'

'Thank you, officer, for telling us,' I said. 'It must be hard to be the bearer of bad news.'

'That it is, sir,' he replied. 'The worse part of our job.'

'What time would we be expected to…to visit the morgue?' I asked, not wanting to say "the body" as I held Alice.

'Any time this morning. Ten o'clock?' he replied.

'We'll be there,' I said, and they both then gave us a salute and left, closing the door behind them and had Alice sobbing on my shoulder. 'Why George? Why him?' she cried, soaking my dressing gown with her tears. There was nothing I could say or do at this moment, only held her tight until she calmed down a little. The front of her gown had opened and I could see one rounded tit there but it didn't arouse me as it might have done under different circumstances.

We sat there for nearly an hour without a word being said, holding her in to my shoulder, feeling her now again giving out a shiver, and with her finally seeming to have calmed down, released her and got up and went into the kitchen to make some coffee.

I'd used mugs and not cups as it would be easier to hold. Even so, with it only half full, her hand shook a couple of times and would have spilt some if it had been full. But she drank it and another mug later as we didn't go back to bed and it wasn't until it was full daylight that I got her to go and have a shower and got dressed, but declined any breakfast when I offered to cook it. So we didn't eat, though I doubt if I could have done so either.

Both having had a shower and gotten dressed, we were back downstairs until it was getting close to 10 that we left the house to go to the morgue. I was surprised at how bright and tastefully decorated it was, expecting it to be gloomy and half in darkness in respect to the dead people that it held. We were directed down a corridor and met by a police officer and a man in a doctor's coat and shown into a small room that had a big window in the opposite wall.

Through this, we could see a shrouded body on a gurney quite close to the glass and another man in a white coat was standing next to each. The man with us knocked on the glass and the one on the other side, pulled down the sheet to uncover the face of George, looking as though he was asleep.

'Is that your husband, George Denton?' the police officer asked of Alice. I was holding her and had felt her sag slightly at seeing his face through the glass.

'Yes,' she whispered, and the other man with us knocked on the glass again and the sheet was pulled back up to cover the face of George. Alice had given out a sob and had quickly turned away from the window, leaning in to me as I held her.

'Sorry, Mrs. Denton. It's hard, I know, but we are required by law for the closest relative to make a positive identification,' the police officer said.

'We understand,' I said, and led Alice out of that room and back to the pick-up for me to drive her home.

'You've got to eat something, Alice,' I said when we were inside. 'Your last meal was dinner.'

'Okay,' she said dully. 'Just a sandwich, Danny.' I went and made four, hoping that she'd at least eat two of them. This she did, which pleased me. 'I…I don't know how I'm going to break the news to Peter,' she said, tears in her eyes.

'I'll do that, Alice,' I said and went into the lounge and picked up the phone and got through to the university, asking them that it was urgent that I spoke to Peter Denton. I was put on hold and had to wait nearly ten minutes before I heard his voice.

'Hello?'

'Peter, it's Danny,' I said.

'Hello, Danny. What's up, ringing me here?' he asked.

'Bad news, Peter. Your dad's dead,' I told him, rather bluntly I know, but how else can you give out bad news?

'Oh Christ!' he exclaimed, and I waited for it to really sink in. 'What…how…how's mom taking it?' he asked and I could hear a sob in his voice.

'She's fine now, though it did hit her when we were told last night,' I said to him.

'Last night? Was it an accident at work?' he asked.

'Not an accident, no. It was a gunfight against four men breaking in to the plant. He shot at least two of them before he was hit. I'm sorry, Peter. So sorry to have to tell you this over the phone, but your mom didn't know how to tell you,' I said.

'I'm coming straight home. Tell her that,' he said.

'Wait a minute, Peter. I'm going to phone the airport and book a ticket for you. Just phone me here on what flight you got and the time of arrival here and I'll meet you,' I told him.

'Oh Danny,' I could hear the tears in his speech. 'Look after mom till I get there.'

'I will, Peter. Sorry to have given you this shock,' I said.

'Well somebody had to and I'm glad that it was you. See you as soon as I can get there,' and with that, the connection was broken. I then phoned the airport he would be using and booked him a ticket, gave them my credit card number and that was then fixed for him to fly home.

'Peter's leaving now,' I told Alice when I got back into the kitchen, 'And I will pick him up when he arrives at the airport.'

'Thank you, Danny. I'm glad you were here when…when we were told, and…and being with me at the morgue. I don't think I would have managed on my own,' she said.

'Why don't you go and lie down? Get some sleep,' I told her.

'I couldn't, no. I…I've got to do something. I've got to get the place clean for when…when…Peter comes home,' she said, I caught that she nearly said George instead of Peter.

'You go and have a sleep,' she said.

'I can't. I'm waiting for Peter to ……' The phone rang, just what I was going to say. I went and picked up the phone.

'Danny?' I heard him ask.

'Yes, Peter, I'm here. What time?' I asked.

'Three hours from now,' he said.

'Fine. I'll be waiting.

'Love you, Danny,' he said.

'Returned,' I said, knowing that he didn't know that Alice knew that we were lovers, not letting him know this over the phone.

So I had two-and-a-half hours before going off to the airport.

'I'm going off to clean up the workshop,' I told Alice, so that's where I spent that time, most of it sitting on the sofa wondering how, with this death of George, the relationship between Alice and myself was going to either develop or disintegrate. Peter was now the equation that had come into our lives in place of George. Where are we going? Something that I mulled over in the workshop and couldn't come up with an answer.

The time came to go to the airport and let Alice know that I was off and got there just before Peter's plane landed. He was the first one to come through the exit from the baggage area and he flung himself into my arms, tears running down his face. We didn't kiss with others seeing us hug each other, though I'm sure some guessed that we were lovers with him crying, them not understanding why.

'Oh Danny,' he had cried.

'Not here, Peter. Not here. Let's get to the pick-up,' I said, breaking free and almost dragging him out of the arrival hall and off to where I was parked. It was only when we were inside did we kiss, him crying again as we kissed and hugged.

'Have you seen him?' he asked, me knowing to what he was referring to.

'Yes. This morning before ringing you. We had to and I held your mother's hand the whole time we were there.'

I broke off the kiss and drove us to his home and upon arrival, saw a strange car there on the drive. I parked and followed Peter indoors where he and Alice almost fell into each other's arms, both crying and I saw two strange gentlemen standing there in the lounge. One of them came forward to me, his hand out.

'You must be Danny Rundene. I'm Wesley Fry, managing director of the plant where Mr. Denton er, worked,' he said. I shook his hand. 'We came here to express our sorrow at the loss of her husband fulfilling his duty as head of security for our plant. We've praised his action in doing his duty, but not in the fact of giving of his life in the name of the company. There's little we can do to replace him in his home with his family, but can help in the loss by giving Mrs. Denton a lifelong pension to help financially with what her husband would have earned if he lived.

A memorial service will be held to honor him and the service he gave to the company, and we will, if acceptable, see to all the finances required for the services at his funeral.

We will also see that his car and any other personal things of his at the plant are returned.'

'Thank you, Mr. Fry, I will pass on what you have said to his wife and son when they have really come to terms with their loss,' I said, and we shook hands and I escorted him and his fellow man who hadn't said a word, out of the house.

Again I offered to cook a meal for Alice and now Peter, but they both refused, but did eventually eat some of the sandwiches that I made. Alice didn't know it, but I had crushed two sleeping tablets and mixed them up in a glass of milk and got her to drink it and got Peter to take her up to her bedroom and see that she went to bed.

I then went to my room and went to bed, not knowing if Peter would come and join me, but he did. He slowly undressed and got into bed with me and turned and went into my arms and cried. Cried at the loss of his father and at how his mother had taken the news and it took a little time to calm him down.

'Has Alice, your mom, gone to sleep?' I asked when he was able to speak and listen to me.

'Yes. I sat there till she went off to sleep, and then came here. The only person I could turn to now. As you are my husband, will you now also be my father?' he said. A strange choice of words but I could see what he meant. He had virtually called me his husband at the motel we had slept at by implying that he was my wife and now he wanted me to become the head of his household. That position was really that of his mother, but I said I would, just to placate him.

'Kiss and make love to me, Danny,' he whispered. 'Fuck me and show me that I'm still alive and not living a dream.'

'That I will, Peter,' I replied and so, had him laying on his back with his legs up high and entered his ass and fucked him. We kissed, still coupled after having cummed inside him, telling him that I loved him as much as he loved me. I didn't miss out that he had laid himself out on his back, the usual position for a woman having sex. Peter, now really proving that he was the "woman" between us. The day had taken its toll on him too, for not long after I had pulled out of him, he too fell asleep.

It took several days for both Peter and Alice to come to terms that George was no longer with us, but the house settled down to the fact and it was really finalised with us, plus at least two hundred other people, attended the funeral. Masses of wreaths and flowers covered the bier in the church for the service. Mr. Fry also saw that there was a sumptuous wake held at the best hotel for all those that had attended the service.

After two hours of people eating and drinking and passing on their condolences to both Alice and Peter, I managed to get everyone's attention by banging on the head table where we were sitting. This I did because I could see that Alice was then looking very tired.

'Ladies and gentlemen. On behalf of Alice, wife of George, and Peter, his son, we thank you all for attending this sorrowful day of losing such a wonderful man, but it has now begun to take its toll on both of them and I thank you, on their behalf, so that they can be excused to return home but beg you to stay to say your own farewells to George at this wake that the plant and Mr. Fry have generously arranged. Thank you all.'

There was a lot of clapping and everybody stopped their eating and drinking to see me escort Alice and Peter out of the hotel's reception room where we'd had the wake.

'Thank you, Danny,' Alice said in the car that drove the three of us home, giving my hand a squeeze. 'I was getting rather tired. It was a lovely speech you gave too, thank you,' and she gave me a kiss which wasn't seen by Peter for he had his head thrown back in the car, his eyes closed.

'It's been a long day and you should go to bed as soon as we get home,' I said.

'I'm glad you are implying that it's your home too, for I don't know how I can now live without you being there,' she said.

'But Peter....?' I started, but stopped. Not knowing how to continue and say the right thing.

'We'll leave that for later, though he should be told some time, but not yet. Let me get my mind around things before we say anything,' which I thought was best too.

On arriving home, I helped her out of the car, waking Peter up for he had fallen asleep, and thanked the driver and as he drove off, helped Alice walk the short distance to get inside the house. She went straight upstairs saying that she was going to bed and I had to help Peter up there as he appeared to have drunk too much and all he could do was flop on my bed I got him there and I took all his clothes off and rolled him over on the bed and covered him before undressing myself and getting into bed with him. No, there wasn't any sex between us that night.

It was a big argument between Alice and Peter at breakfast the next morning. Peter wanted to leave the university and start working to bring money into the house. Alice put her foot down and said that he would earn a damn sight more at having a degree in his field. Besides, she was getting a decent pension that would be more than enough, besides, I, she said, was already paying my way in respect of food so there was no need for him to give up his future.

Of course, Peter tried to drag me into the argument but I had to take his mother's side in saying that she was right.

'I thought you would stick up for me,' Peter said in a whining tone.

'I do stick up for you most of the time, Peter,' I said, seeing a smirk from Alice at those words of mine. 'But on this, I agree with Alice.' He slumped back, knowing his argument had been defeated. It was a truculent look I got from him by not being on his side.

I had not taken on any work since the death of George and I wouldn't until Peter had gone back to the university and I felt that Alice would be alright at home alone. You might ask how Alice came to be at home when she had been a school teacher. With Peter going off to university and me staying, she packed up to become a housewife, also with George having changed his job due to the accident with his hand was the main reason, or so she had said at the time. But I had my doubts on her remarks being the real reason.

That night, Alice knew that Peter would be in bed with me and so said an early goodnight to leave us alone downstairs as she went up to a lonely bed. Peter was soon in my arms on the sofa downstairs, kissing me and feeling that I had an erection inside my trousers.

'Take me to bed, Danny, and fuck me with what I can feel. Fuck your wife and give me a baby,' he said. Shades of the Winters. Him wanting to become pregnant! No chance with nature as it was. No male had so far given birth and none would be likely to either.

'Do you really believe that you are my wife?' I asked him.

'Yes,' was the simple reply. 'I do. I love your cock, not only to suck but have up inside me. I love you being on top with your hard cock inside me, giving me more pleasure than anything else here on Earth.' What could I say to that? I could have argued that he was a man and not a woman, but seeing that determined look on his face, didn't, so it was something that I had to accept for I loved him. I love fucking him and in return, he could fuck me, something a real woman couldn't do, so that was the way it was going to be.

So with that, we went up to bed where I fucked him as a woman with him lying on his back and after I had cum inside him, had him fuck me as a man, being on my knees and having him take me from the rear. We later had oral sex as only men could do, sucking on each other's cock and taking in the cum to savor and swallow. We also fucked each other in the morning before having our shower and breakfast and me taking him to the airport where I bought his ticket and took him into the toilets where we could have a kiss goodbye.

'He got off alright?' Alice asked when I returned to the house.

'Yes, and he said that you were right in what you had said,' I lied, 'That he had to finish at the university and get his degree.' She gave me a kiss.

'It's not what I envisaged or wanted, but it's happened and now I have you all to myself, Danny,' she said kissing me again. 'Take me to bed.'

I took her hand and we went upstairs but was pulled away from the door of my room and, for the first time, took me into her room. The room that she had used to sleep with George. This then was the binding moment of our relationship, by taking me to her own bed that she no longer shared with George.

It didn't take us long to be naked and on her bed, to kiss and play with each other until I took over and went down to taste once again, what juices would come out of her pussy. There was more when she had her orgasm that I took into my mouth and then mounted her and brought her up to another one with me cumming inside her at the same time.

So with me fucking her on her own bed, I was now, not only a husband to her son Peter, but also a surrogate husband to her. A position that I had never thought I would be in, but, c'est la vie. With Peter now back at the university, I started working full time again, working during the day and coming home after work to be greeted by my surrogate wife and then, after dinner, going to bed for us to make love.

It was an idyllic period until Peter came home for his holiday. Then things changed, though not in any way that we would have thought of. He came by bus from the university because of his baggage and I duly collected him from the bus station and drove him home. We had kissed in the car but that was all at the time. We duly arrived where he was greeted by his mother with a kiss on the cheek and a hug while I took his things upstairs.

I had not taken on any work this day and so we had lunch with Peter telling Alice how he was progressing with his studies, which pleased her. After we had eaten, He wanted to go out to the workshop and I saw the grin on Alice's face as he said this, her knowing full well that it was for sex that Peter wanted me to go there with him. I gave a shrug of my shoulders for her benefit and followed him out into the garden.

As soon as we were inside, Peter was in my arms kissing me.

'I've been completely faithful this term and I'm hungry for you, Danny,' he said, starting to undress me till I was naked and sporting an erection. 'This is what I've been missing,' he said, handling my throbbing cock and going down onto his knees and sucking on me.

'Not too much, Peter, if you want me to fuck you,' I said, prying his head off of my cock.

'I do, I do,' he cried, getting up and quickly taking his clothes off to be as naked as I was, his cock up hard too, like mine. He threw himself onto the sofa, on his back with his legs wide open as were his arms. 'Come and fuck me, husband,' he said. 'Come and fuck your wife.'

When I had made sure that the workshop was clean and tidy the day before, I had opened a window for the place to be aired and now I wished I had shut it, for I caught a glimpse of Alice being outside and from the look on her face, had heard what Peter had said. But it had been said now and there wasn't a thing I could do about it. She'd seen me fuck him before so I had no compunction in getting between his legs and lifting them up to my shoulders, lifting his ass up at the same time before poking the head of my cock inside him.

'Lovely husband! Lovely,' he cried as I pushed myself all the way into him until I could go no further. His hands had come up to hold my shoulders, his face positively beaming as he felt my cock twitching away inside him and his muscle flexing itself round the shaft of my cock. He crooned away as I fucked him, loving the tightness of his ass in this position as I ploughed it. But my need for release was great and was soon ramming up hard into him and began shooting my cum for him to feel each shot to which he gave out gurgles as he smiled up at me.

With me coming to a stop, he eased his legs off my shoulders for them to slip down to my sides and for me to fall forward for him to hold and kiss while my cock is still inside him. I was squashing his erect cock so didn't want to move myself and have him cum between our stomachs, for I wanted him to fuck me too. With his legs sliding down straight and his body relaxing, I felt myself slipping out of that tight hole I'd just fucked and got a cry from him as I left his hot and tight ass. He gave me another fierce kiss.

'My turn now to fuck my husband and lover,' he said, making me wince for I was sure that Alice was still outside of the window and could clearly hear what he had said. I lifted myself up off of him and got up and went to the small sink there and washed my cock before returning to the sofa where I got on and stayed on my knees with my ass in the air, seeing his swaying cock move out of sight as he got behind me.

My body gave out that lovely tremor when I felt the head of his erection touch the entrance to my body and with his hands on my hips, felt him push forward and had his throbbing cock slide nice and easily up into my ass. Such was his need for release, there wasn't much between him moving his cock back and forth inside me that he began to really ram into me and then shooting out his cum to coat my insides, giving me the extra pleasure of feeling it do so.

He came to a stop, leaning heavily over my rear end, his cock still throbbing away before he straightened up and pulled out of me. Like him, I too gave out a small cry at feeling that lovely fucking tool leaving me, really wanting it pushed back into me. But he got off the sofa and went and washed himself before coming back to fall into my arms for us to kiss and have our tongues talk to each other.

We didn't go any further than that and soon broke apart and got dressed before leaving the workshop and going back into the house.

'Have fun in there?' Alice asked with a smile. I didn't rise up to the bait but Peter did.

'Fine. Just seeing that everything was okay and in the right place,' he said.

Christ! He's coming out with innuendos, I thought and Alice picked it up with a smile.

'Yes,' I said, jumping in before Alice could add another one. 'The only thing I forgot yesterday was to shut the window,' and shaking my head at her. She got the message and didn't carry on.

The rest of the day went smoothly right up and through dinner and the shit didn't hit the fan until we were in bed.

I turned in first, having a shower before getting into bed and waited for Peter. I heard Peter's door close and knew that he would stay there until he knew that his mother had gone to bed, which was about 30 minutes after Peter had entered his room. So it was another 15 minutes before my door opened, quietly and closed the same when Peter came in. He was wearing a dressing gown and quickly dropped it and got onto bed with me. Both of us had erections in anticipation of using them on each other as he came straight into my arms and kissed me.

'In bed again, for the whole six weeks,' he said, bubbling over at the exciting thought of having sex every night. 'I've be looking forward so long for this. Fuck me first, Danny.'

He rolled off of me and lay on his back ready for me to get between his open legs. 'It's a lovely sight, seeing your cock sticking out like that knowing that it's for me.' He lifted his legs up as I moved in closer, having his heels land on my shoulders first and then slide up till it was his lower calves that rested there as I leaned over his body, supporting myself on outstretched rigid arms. His smile turned briefly to a grimace as I expanded his asshole with the head of my cock until it slid inside him to bring back the smile on his face.

Neither of us heard the bedroom door open or close as I was now fucking Peter. Also, not having eyes in the back of my head, couldn't see Alice approach the bottom of the bed. Peter couldn't see her either with my body in the way and having his eyes fixed on my face. I was just reaching my peak when Alice spoke.

'So my son Peter's being fucked by his husband.' I went rigid but couldn't help shooting out my cum into Peter's ass at hearing her voice behind me. Peter's eyes went wide and he gasped, whether it was from feeling my cum hit his insides or now seeing his mother's face looming over my shoulder, I don't know.

'Mom!' he gasped, his legs slipping off my shoulders as she moved around to one side of the bed. 'You...you shouldn't be in here!'

'Nor should you, but you're here and now so am I,' she said. Peter's face was now pure white and he seemed to be struggling to pull himself back and make me slip out of him. I glanced down and saw that his cock had now deflated and lying rather limp on his stomach. 'So the "husband" is fucking his "wife",' she said, 'being fucked by my lover.'

Oh shit, I said to myself, feeling my own cock rapidly losing its strength, now she's gone and done it!

'Wha...wha...yo...your lover?' he gasped out with a stutter. 'Your lover?'

'After things had settled down after your father died, yes. Danny became my lover, for I need a man now with your father gone and you are not going to monopolise him.' My cock had now slipped right out of Peter and I sat back on my heels, feeling my face being red as opposed to the whiteness of Peter's.

'Go and wash yourself, Danny,' she said to me, and so I got off the bed and went into the bathroom but could still hear what was being said.

'How...how or where did you get the husband -wife thing from?' I heard Peter ask.

'From your own mouth when you were in the workshop this afternoon. The window was open,' she told him.

'You saw us then?' he asked.

'I've seen the two of you fucking each other for a couple of years now, it was only today that I've learned that you now consider yourself to be the "wife" between you two,' she answered him.

'For two years?' he cried. 'For two years you've known and never said a word?'

'No. Why should I? It's your life and if you liked being fucked and fucking him, why should I interfere? But with us losing your father and now not having a man, I seduced Danny into having sex with me. You liked it and he is well hung, so I wanted it as much as you do,' she told him.

I walked back into the bedroom to see that Alice was now sitting on the edge of the bed, Peter still lying on his back.

'Danny!' he cried on seeing me. 'You…you've been fucking my mom?'

'Yes,' I mumbled.

'Why? Why my mom?' he cried again.

'Well you were at the university. I was alone, your mom was alone, well, er, it just happened,' I said.

'I was being faithful to you,' he said, anguish on his face.

'You only told me this on this return. You had played around there before, so I thought you still were, so what's good for the goose, is good enough for the gander,' I shot back at him.

'Oh hell! What do we do now?' he cried.

'Carry on as before,' Alice said. 'He fucks you. He fucks me. We both suck on his cock and you get to fuck him, something I can't do. Oh, he also sucks and licks my pussy,' she added as an afterthought.

'But…but,' began, stuttering. 'It's not right!'

'It's not right that you two fuck each other either, but you do. So I want what is right, it being a man and a woman coupling.'

'But it's still not right! You're my mom,' he cried, and she was quick in her riposte.

'It's not right with you being my son!' she shot back at him. I was keeping out of this for the moment, waiting to see who was going to collapse first and my money was on Peter giving in. I won my mental bet.

'So…so when, er, when do you want him?' Peter asked, knowing that he had lost the argument.

'Is this a game you're playing, Alice?' I whispered just before she kissed me.

'It might be, but I'm laying down the law as to when and how we have sex together,' she whispered back.

'So I'm the piggy in the middle? I asked.

'No. You're bigger than that. More of being a rooster that fucks the mother hen and will still let you fuck her chick,' she said just before Peter came back into the bedroom.

Kiss me, Danny.' So I did. 'You now have two "wives."

'What about Peter?' I asked.

'Well he now has a "husband" and I, a lover,' was the reply.

I had no answer to this.

So that's how it was for the weeks that Peter was home. Then he went back to the university and it was back to just Alice and myself having sex until he would come home again. He still has another two years of studying before he graduates. What we would do when the time came? We had no idea for that was in the future.

Meanwhile, I just loved being here at Peter's house.

THE END

Here is a sample from another story you may enjoy:

AMY REDEK

The
Wizard
of Kos

Erotic Fantasy

Milos Drake was and had been a wizard for the past sixty years and came from a family of wizards that had always lived in the village of Hazelwood.

He was young for his age for the average life of the wizards in the village was four hundred years, give or take a few decades. Unless, like in the case of his parents, some unforeseen accident occurs like trying a new spell to transport themselves to another village. Something went wrong and they were never seen again.

That had happened twenty years earlier, and ever since, the other wizards of the village had worked on this and finally made a success of it, but though many of them travelled the length and breadth of the country, they never found the parents of Milos. So at the tender age of forty, he became an orphan and lived alone with just his inside and outside elves.

As it implies, the inside elf look after everything inside of the house while the outside elf saw to the garden, vegetable patch and the upkeep of the outside of the house.

The inside elf wore an orange smock while the outside elf wore a green one. The colours never varied and they were known respectively as Quirk and Quarrel. They were aptly named for Quirk, the inside elf had the tendency to never put things back in their right places and a habit of mishearing whatever order he was given.

Quarrel, the outside elf would nearly always pick an argument with Quirk when a specific vegetable was required. He hadn't planted them yet; they were not yet fully grown; they'd been eaten by fly pests, whatever. He was always trying to pick an argument with Quirk who had become wise to him and would ask for things like turquip beans or fantail radishes just to set him off.

In spite of the hassles those two had together, Milos was well looked after and never ever really wanted anything else, except the one thing that any young man desired, and that was the company of a female.

Now you might say that sixty years of age was getting a bit past the time of wanting a young woman but you must realise that they lived for nearly four hundred years and so by any human standards of life, he was only just reaching his prime.

Besides, they didn't normally marry until they were a hundred years old as a rule and even then, the village kept control over the birth rate to maintain a steady flow of growing wizards so as not to exceed the number that could be contained within the village.

There were three other young male wizards of his age and four female ones, and when he reached the age of ninety, he was expected to start courting one of these females with the intention of marriage and continuing the life of the village.

But he had not been under any parental control for the past twenty years and so began to take liberties as far as the women folk of the village were concerned. He was a handsome man and looked quite virile and had a likeable charm about him that soon had woman falling over themselves for him. The best part for him was that he didn't have to use any magical incantations or things like that, it was just his own charm that wooed them to become like putty in his hands.

He knew the theory of having sex with a woman but had not as such been able to get onto the practical side until he came across Lilith Buckfaster. She was a buxom girl of his own age and they had attended wizard school together as had the other three girls and boys of their age. She was one of the four girls that he would be expected to be married to when the time came, but he was too anxious to wait that long.

He found her out in one of the surrounding meadows one fine day, searching through the grass.

'Hello Lilith, what are you looking for?' he asked, walking over to where she was moving the grass about with a stick.

'I'm looking for some worzel fungus for a potion I'm making,' she replied, bending down as she looked at the ground. He could see her firm breasts inside the bodice she was wearing and felt himself start to stir at the sight…

If you enjoyed this sample then look for **The Wizard of Kos**.

Also by this Author

About the Author

I have always been a hard worker my whole life. I concentrated so much on building a career in business, getting higher degrees, that I forgot how to cultivate my younger dreams.

Writing is a passion that I have pushed aside in a little blue corner in my New York apartment. When I moved to Australia to work for a big company, I realized that I needed to rediscover my passion for writing again.

Writing. Passion. Erotica.

There's just something about men in women's clothes, men on top and bottoms that fascinate me. It touches a spot in which an undiscovered burning desire is yet to be kindled with.

From the Author

Check my page on Amazon and my blog for Updates and interesting info.

Author Central - http://www.amazon.com/Amy-Redek/e/B00A48NQ72
Author Blog - http://amy-redek.awesomeauthors.org/

If you enjoyed any of my books then please share the love and click like on my books in Amazon.

If you write me a review and send me an email I will send you a free book, or many.
(Just know that these emails are filtered by my publisher.)

Good news is always welcome.

One Last Thing, For Kindle Readers...

When you turn the page, Kindle will give you the opportunity to rate this book and share your thoughts on Facebook and Twitter. If you enjoyed my writings, would you please take a few seconds to let your friends know about it? Because... when they enjoy they will be grateful to you and so will I.

Thank You!

Amy Redek
amy_redek@awesomeauthors.org